from the

Underhills

THE CAMBRIDGE CAPER

THE CAMBRIDGE CAPER

Thomas W. Underhill

iUniverse, Inc.

New York Lincoln Shanghai

The Cambridge Caper

iUniverse books may be ordered through booksellers or by contacting:

iUniverse
2021 Pine Lake Road, Suite 100
Lincoln, NE 68512
www.iuniverse.com
1-800-Authors (1-800-288-4677)

ISBN-13: 978-0-595-37231-7 (pbk)
ISBN-13: 978-0-595-81629-3 (ebk)
ISBN-10: 0-595-37231-7 (pbk)
ISBN-10: 0-595-81629-0 (ebk)

Printed in the United States of America

Foreword

My father, Thomas W. Underhill, read to me constantly when I was little. As my brother and I grew older, Dad read aloud some of his favorite mysteries, among which were *The Hound of the Baskervilles* and *The Journeying Boy*. He is directly responsible for my addiction to reading and becoming a mystery writer myself.

Tom Underhill was a graduate of Princeton University (class of 1944) and Harvard Law School (1949). He worked as patent lawyer for the Kendall Company in Chicago and Boston and the Monsanto Co. in St. Louis. *The Cambridge Caper* was written during the 1970s, based in part on his recollections of law school in the late 1940s. During his retirement Dad wrote another legal mystery novel and numerous crossword puzzles, some of which were published in the New York Times Magazine. My father died at his home on Cape Cod in 2003 without seeing either manuscript become a published book.

It has been my pleasant task to make Dad's work available using print-on-demand technology. My brother Nicholas K. Underhill of Cleveland, OH, shared the cost of this venture and I served as editor. The story is essentially as my father wrote it, with some very minor changes.

We dedicate this novel to Janet Means Underhill, our beloved stepmother.

Sarah Underhill Wisseman
Champaign, Illinois, September 2005.

CHAPTER 1

▼

The 707 banked over the water on its approach to Logan airport in East Boston. Charlie Witherspoon fastened his seat belt and latched the seat in its upright position. The space fore and aft was really not adequate for his six foot-six frame. To make matters worse, there had been a tie-up in the so-called "express" lane on the way to O'Hare in Chicago. He'd made his plane with only minutes to spare. The flight was full, and as the last person to check in, he'd been assigned a center seat at the extreme rear of the plane in the smoking section. As a non-smoker Charlie hated the location and wasn't sure he could make it to Boston without gagging. The worst was yet to come. He was sandwiched between the parents of an unhappy small baby. The parents weren't so happy either. They hadn't bought a seat for the baby but had been planning to park him in the space where Charlie now sat.

Witherspoon at thirty-eight still had a boyish air about him. He had a full head of hair, as bushy as Teddy Kennedy's in his prime. His weight remained the same 180 pounds it had been when he was eighteen and had reached his full height. If it were not for his immaculate, three-piece, worsted suit, solid red linen tie and the solemn touch added by horned-rim glasses, he might have been taken for a college sophomore. In fact, he had just been made a partner in one of Chicago's top law firms. The suit was not really immaculate. It would have been if the baby had not burped copiously on his right sleeve, much to the amusement of its parents.

*   *   *   *

The cab came out of the tunnel and went up the ramp leading to Storrow Drive and Cambridge. Even at three p.m. on a Thursday, the traffic was already heavy. Charlie shuddered to think what it would be like in another two hours.

He had come a day early for his tenth reunion at Harvard Law School, traveling tourist class to save money when he could afford the best. Next time, when the client was paying, he'd go first class. His nephew, Tom Endicott, had pressed him to come early to help celebrate the end of the second year law exams. Charlie checked into the room he had reserved at the Commander Hotel. The rooms were small compared to those in the newer motels, but the Commander was convenient to Harvard Square and the Law School. Charlie had no desire to drive in the city, and the warm May weather was perfect for walking.

The phone rang. Since he had already talked to his nephew from the airport, it must be Sid Rosenblatt calling, the only other person who knew he would be in Cambridge a day early.

"Hello, Charlie? This is Rosie. I hope you're still planning to have dinner with me tonight. There's a new French restaurant with superb food within walking distance of your hotel."

"Fine, Rosie. I'm going to a student party near Central Square after dinner. You're invited if you can put up with students outside of class."

"It wouldn't be the first time," said Rosie. He was on leave from Columbia to do a one-year stint teaching evidence at Harvard. "I've already made a reservation at the restaurant. I'll pick you up at your hotel a little after seven. That will give us plenty of time for a leisurely dinner. I assume the party's at your nephew's place. Nothing really happens there until ten when the crashers begin to show up."

Le Plat D'Argent was everything Rosie said it was. The coq au vin was as good as the best Charlie had eaten—at *Chez Tante Louise* in Paris. That was before Henry Kissinger had popularized the place by taking his dates there. The wine, a 1969 Chateau Margaux, was sinfully expensive but worth every penny.

Charlie felt a wave of nostalgia as they climbed the stairs from the subway at Central Square. He and Rosie walked north to Austin Street and then west past the YWCA. In Charlie's day as a law student, if you didn't know your date well enough to ask her to share your bed, you could put her up at the "Y" for five dollars instead of the twenty you'd have to pay at a hotel. Charlie also remembered a pick-up basketball game on the Y's undersized court. He'd been high scorer with six points.

Across the street from the Y was the duplex apartment Charlie had shared with eleven other law students ten years ago.

The red brick had been sandblasted to make it look almost respectable. The sagging rear staircase where Charlie had kissed his first Radcliffe girl had been replaced and freshly painted. The neighborhood had improved. The tricycle near the stairwell meant children and an upper middle class family to afford the rents, if in fact anyone paid rent. Probably the apartments of Charlie's day had been converted to condominiums to get around Cambridge rent controls.

As they approached the two hundred block on Inman Avenue, the noise level took a quantum jump. Someone was shouting from an open window, "Offeree, offeror, Hahvad, Hahvad, Hahvad Lor."

Must be a local, thought Charlie. They leave out the R's where they are and put them in where they aren't. He half expected to see the riot squad pull up at 236.

Tom Endicott was just inside the door as they arrived. The family resemblance was uncanny. Except for his blond hair, worn almost shoulder length in the fashion of the seventies, Tom was a younger edition of Charlie.

Charlie glanced at the small table with the telephone near the front door. Yes, the book *Five Hundred Delinquent Women* was still there. Co-authored by Sheldon Glueck, one-time professor of criminal law and his wife, Eleanor—she was also an authority on the criminal mind—the book contained some fascinating case histories. To the dismay of the prurient, there was little delinquency of a sexual nature. Charlie had found the book as a law student and kept it in his apartment as a conversation piece. He'd passed it on to his nephew.

Tom Endicott spoke, "Charlie, that book still draws a lot of attention. Some idiots even write in it." Rosie picked up the book and leafed through it at random. Telephone numbers and comments appeared: "8.5 on a scale of 10" and "See 210 S.W." had been added.

"I don't understand the citation," said Rosie. "I know it means Volume 210 of the Southwestern Reporter, but what page?"

Charlie laughed. "You must be one of the innocents, Rosie. Generations of law students have feasted on the explicit sex reported in that court decision. You don't need to know the page number to look it up in the Langdell Library. The volume automatically falls open to the right page when you pick it up."

On the other side of the doorway stood a dilapidated upright piano. Peter van Pelt, one of Tom's roommates, managed to make it sound like a Steinway. He was surrounded by a group singing surprisingly good four-part harmony. Charlie recognized the strains of *Aura Lee.*

"I haven't heard that one in a long time," he said. "Reminds me of my college days."

Making introductions along the way, Tom led Charlie and Rosie to the kitchen to pour them drinks from a bottle carefully labeled with his name. This was a BYOL party. There were already a half a dozen dead soldiers in the trash can.

Someone had made an effort to clean up for the party. The dishes had been washed and put away on the shelves for a change. The floor looked swept. The top of the stove showed signs of a lick and a promise, but there were places where the spilled food had hardened to the consistency of concrete. Charlie was willing to bet that the oven had not been cleaned within the memory of man.

Tom saw his uncle's appraising glance at the stove and smiled. "There's something else you should see. Come with me."

They left Rosie talking to two students in the living room and went back through the hall to the bedroom area. Tom opened a door and switched on an overhead light. One of the twin beds was crowned with an incredible heap of dirty clothes, law books, notebooks and various odds and ends including a battered naval officer's raincoat that looked like a relic of World War II.

"That's Kevin's bed," Tom said. "Kevin Flaherty has five older sisters who have spoiled him rotten. He's never had to pick up for himself before, and there have been no signs that he's going to start now. He's the only one of us in his third year, but you'd never know it. His sister Kathleen, who lives in Cambridge, comes by once a week to collect his laundry and pick up for him. This week her husband was sick, and she didn't make it. He left a trail of litter in every room. We couldn't even get him to clean up for the party. We finally dumped all of his leavings on his bed except the dirty glasses, which we washed for the party. There were two glasses under his bed that must have been there six months."

"Where will he put all that junk when he goes to bed?" asked Charlie.

"The last time this happened, he completely ignored the pile. He just crawled into bed under it and slept like a log. Of course he had put away the better part of a fifth of whiskey—good Old Guggenslocker as I recall."

They went back to the living room where Tina Forbes, a Radcliffe junior, was the center of attraction in a group of law students. She was Tom's date for the evening as she had been at least twice a week over the past two months. Her peaches and cream complexion was set off by a mass of flaming red hair. She was telling a story about the Holyoke Medical Center, using lots of body language.

"There I was in the waiting room when this slip of a girl came out of an inner office followed by one of the nurses. The girl couldn't have been more than seventeen, just your type, Tom. The nurse said, 'Are you sure no one else has been exposed? If there is anyone else, he ought to get treatment, you know.' The girl thought a moment and said, 'No.' Then she stopped as she got to the door, smiling reflectively as something occurred to her. 'Do quickies count?' she asked."

The audience roared.

"Hey, Tina, why were *you* there?" Tom asked.

"None of your business," said Tina, adding to herself, "at least not yet."

In the opposite corner of the room, two nearly besotted men were drinking to the various subdivisions of the city of Newton. Since there are a dozen or more, the road to complete inebriation promised to be a rapid one. Tom thought of a footnote in the Criminal Law Casebook he had used twelve years ago:

"He is not drunk who from the floor
Can rise again and drink once more;
But he is drunk who prostrate lies
And who can neither drink nor rise."

One of the drinkers was a third-year student, John Rogers, who lived in the downstairs apartment. The other was a middle-aged man with an unsavory air about him. Tom knew who he was but wanted to forget. He wondered which one of his roommates had asked him to the party.

The unsavory one raised his glass. "Here's to Newtonville," he said.

"Newton Center," came the reply toast.

"West Newton." Two more slugs went down the hatch.

"Newton Lower Falls!"

"Newton Upper Falls!"

"Up her what?" asked one of the lunatics on the fringe of the toasting. The unsavory one said, "Waban," drained a half-full glass, and collapsed to the floor. The law student, who seemed to have unlimited capacity, finished his toast to Waban, which really is one of the Newtons, then felt the urge to telephone someone. His candidate was the Swedish tenor, Ussi Berling, currently appearing at La Scala. He rushed to the phone and dialed M-I-L-A-N. Tom, who had been watching the performance, knew that John Rogers was beyond his limit. He took him gently by the arm. "Come on, now, John. It's time to go to bed. You always start making long distance phone calls when you're tanked. The last time you did try it cost you fifty bucks." Tom helped him down the stairs to his bed, covered him with a blanket, and went back up to the party.

He found Tina draping a bed sheet over the fallen toaster. Tina said, "Charlie's been reminiscing about his career as a professional Harvard man. I can't believe that anyone could put in four years at the college, two at the business school, two at the medical school and then top it off with three years here to get a law degree."

"Remember there was a financial incentive," said Charlie, "thanks to my grandfather's spendthrift trust. $25,000 a year tax-free so long as I was a student in good standing at some part of the university."

Across the room Kevin Flaherty was talking to a well-endowed Wellesley type who exaggerated what she already had by thrusting it out to be admired. Kevin was really not concentrating on the conversation. Only five-six, he was standing on tiptoe to examine as much cleavage as he possibly could. He was also calculating whether her bust measurement lived up to her advance billing. As if reading his mind, Beverly reached into her purse, pulled out a cloth tape measure and handed it to him. "Measure for yourself, 38-24-36."

It was three a.m. when the tumult and shouting died and the last guest departed. Except for the labored breathing of the character sleeping it off under the sheet in the living room, and the giggles coming from under the pile of junk on Kevin's bed, everything was quiet at 236 Inman Avenue.

CHAPTER 2

▼

Tom Endicott was by nature the neatest of the law students who shared the apartment. After he put water on the stove in the morning for coffee, he went around picking up empty glasses and full ashtrays. In the living room he noticed the sheet was still there, covering the form of the man who had been drinking to the Newtons. He picked up the sheet and as he was folding it looked more closely at the supine figure. There was no motion in the chest, no sign of breathing. The eyes bulged, the skin felt cold to the touch and he could find no pulse at all. Tom knew it was too late for first-aid measures, but he tried old-fashioned artificial respiration—the only kind he knew—and shouted to rouse his roommates. Pete van Pelt staggered out into the room in his skivvies, a hangover from a stretch in the navy. He looked like death warmed over but he managed to take in what Tom was telling him. He dialed the police emergency number and spoke briefly to someone at the other end of the line; then he did a double take.

"Christ!" he said. "That Wellesley dish is still shacked up with Kevin. We've got to get her out of here before the police come." He pulled on a pair of khaki trousers and pounded on the door of the bedroom across the hall. Phil Roberts, who shared the room with Kevin, was in the infirmary with a case of mumps.

"Get dressed, both of you!" he yelled. "We're expecting the police any minute."

"What's up?" asked Kevin in a blurry voice, still half asleep. In the background there was a low, vibrant laugh.

"No time to explain. Get that refugee from Munger stables out of here for her own good." He pushed open the door to hurry things up. Beverly was already on her feet. She picked up some clothes and headed for the bathroom, not the least embarrassed by her nudity. Pete noticed the mass of junk they had piled on Kevin's bed before the party had been moved to a desk some time during the night.

"So you finally found an incentive to move that stuff?" he said.

"Where shall we go?" asked Kevin, at last beginning to move. "Downstairs?"

"Not far enough. The police are sure to check down there. Take her to the Honeybee for breakfast. Here's some cash. Call in here in about an hour to see if the coast is clear. Ask for yourself. If the police are still here, I'll say, 'Sorry, Kevin's gone out. Can I take a message?'"

Tom Endicott watched from the window. Kevin and Beverly were safely out on the street and well away from the apartment entrance when the police ambulance drove up.

The driver made a quick examination of the body and asked to use the phone. The second policeman stood around looking useless.

"Cambridge police. Lynch calling. Connect me with Homicide,"

The voice on the phone was loud that Tom could hear every word.

"Homicide, Detective Sergeant Libertino."

"Joe, this is Bill Lynch. They've got me driving the goddamed ambulance again. Hennessey is down with the flu. I've got a dead one here at 236 Inman Avenue. Looks like he was smothered, but that's for the M.E. to say."

"I'll come over myself," said the voice. "Wait for me and make sure nothing's disturbed."

✳   ✳   ✳   ✳

Joe Libertino was not the man on the street's idea of an Italian. His father came from Lombardy in the north of Italy. His blond hair, blue eyes and pale complexion made most people jump to the conclusion he was Scandinavian. He showed up at Inman Avenue with a crew that included a photographer and a fingerprint man. The medical examiner arrived ten minutes later.

After the body had been removed, Libertino started questioning the students in the room shared by Endicott and van Pelt. He sent one of his men downstairs to round up the five law students who lived there. A tape recorder whirred in the background.

No one admitted knowing the dead man. Libertino realized the eight students who lived in the building were only a beginning. If he could believe his ears, there had been more than 100 people at the party. He wondered whether it was going to be possible to get an accurate list.

The dead man's wallet showed him to be Lawrence Fisher. In addition to a driver's license, the wallet contained only fifteen dollars and a couple of credit cards. Libertino knew Fisher by reputation only. He had been a brilliant criminal lawyer until a conviction for income tax evasion had led to disbarment. He now specialized in peddling influence, one of the sleazy types who hang around City Hall and the State House. Libertino recalled hearing that Fisher also picked up a few bucks by tutoring law students. So far Libertino had no success in finding out how Fisher happened to be at the party.

Tom Endicott said, "It's really not surprising, Sergeant. Our parties have become famous. Perhaps notorious is a better word. There are always a few gate-crashers. We don't mind so long as they bring their own booze and don't tear up the place too much."

"Don't tell me again about those three babes from Newtonville," said Libertino. "Your buddy here, van Pelt, claims they just called up out of the blue asking to come to a party they'd heard about in a bar."

"It's the gospel truth. I took the call myself. I warned them they'd have to provide their own transportation both ways. Somehow I got the impression they were planning to spend the night. Later I wondered why they bothered to call in advance. They could have just showed up and no one would have asked any questions."

*   *   *   *

When the police left, Tom got out the checks his roommates had given him the day before and prepared to go to the bank. He hadn't wanted the job of handling the finances for the gang of them, but no one else had volunteered to do anything about the absolute chaos of the first two months of living together. There were bitter arguments about whose food was whose. They kept four opened quarts of milk in the refrigerator—at least two of them usually sour. Tom had been forced to hide his beer outside his bedroom window, a trick that van Pelt had discovered all too soon. Now they had communal food and beer. Everyone kept rough track of his consumption on a chart in the kitchen and gave Tom a monthly check in advance to cover the rent, utilities, food and beer and to make the necessary adjustments for unequal consumption. The system wasn't perfect, but it worked—as long as they remembered not to let Kevin do the shopping. He came back one time with whole coffee beans. There were still arguments over the

utility bills when some of them stayed in the apartment over a law school vacation while others went home. Fortunately they all had jobs in Boston that summer, with a full-time job for Kevin.

Tom filled out a deposit slip at the Central Square branch of the Harvard
Trust Company. He really looked at the checks for the first time and burst out
laughing. One was made out to "Mickey Mouse," the second, "Care of One Barrel of Beer.'" The third was conventional. Phil Roberts had even managed to mail
his check from the Infirmary. He noted the third check was drawn on the Harvard Trust Company. He endorsed the checks, adding above his signature on the
back of the third check "For identification only".

The teller, Maria Ardito, was a sweet young thing who had just started with
the bank a month ago. Tom felt almost sorry for her.

"Good morning, Mr. Endicott," she said. Her jaw dropped as she examined
the checks carefully. "'Mickey Mouse,' 'One Barrel of Beer.' Oh, dear. What am
I supposed to do with these?"

The line behind Tom was beginning to build up. A lot of people tried to fit
their banking needs into the lunch hour. Tom couldn't have picked a worse time
to tie up the line. The branch manager looked over from his desk and frowned. It
was unfortunate that the head teller was out sick.

Tom Endicott was stubborn. He said, "Under the Uniform Negotiable Instru-
ments Law a check made out to an object or to a fictitious person is payaole to
bearer. You'll admit that Mickey Mouse is a fictitious person, won't you?"

She nodded in resignation, then looked at the endorsement on the third
check. "What does this mean, Mr. Endicott, 'For identification only'?"

"I used that endorsement because you're the drawee bank," he said.

"I'm the what?" She recoiled as if he had made an obscene suggestion.

The manager arrived at the tail end of this conversation. He knew it was the
policy of the bank to humor law students, at least up to a point. They could make
a lot of trouble if they weren't handled fairly. Then there was always the possibility that some of them would stay in the area as lawyers and remember the friendly
bank that had put up with their pranks.

"What's the matter, Miss Ardito?" he asked.

"Mr. Williams, look at these checks Mr. Endicott is trying to deposit."

After studying the checks, Williams barely repressed a chuckle. "Put them
through, Miss Ardito. If he wanted cash, I'd have to check with the legal department. This way there's no risk. Two of the checks are drawn on the First
National. It's their worry whether to honor them. We'll just make sure that they
clear before permitting Mr. Endicott to use any of the deposit. The third check

with the unusual endorsement is drawn on our bank. All that Mr. Endicott is try-ing to avoid is any liability as an endorser. Quite right, too. It's our responsibility to detect any forgery and make sure there are sufficient funds."

CHAPTER 3

▼

Tom picked up Tina at Lowell House and they headed for the grassy banks of the Charles. It was a perfect day for a picnic, temperature in the mid-seventies, only a few scattered clouds in a buttermilk sky and just enough wind to keep the bugs away. They were able to find a sheltered spot near the boathouse. There were turkey sandwiches on homemade whole-wheat bread, a couple of apples and a decent California Chablis.

"I still can't believe that man was killed in your apartment last night," she said. "Are you sure it couldn't have been an accident?"

"I'm afraid it has to be murder," replied Tom. "It's possible for a grown man to smother himself, I suppose. He'd have to be very drunk, which this one was, but then there wouldn't have been the signs of a struggle. He must have come to as someone held a pillow over his face. It wouldn't take much strength to do it. Even you might have managed."

Tina shuddered. "Why did it have to happen at your place?"

"Probably sheer opportunism. Anyone at the party could have stayed until we went to bed, or left the building to come back later when everything was quiet. I've opened the outside door into the vestibule with a credit card myself. It's no trick at all. There is a bolt, but we never use it. When you come in late at night, it's just too much trouble to check whether everyone else is in. Someone did bolt the door once. A Johnny-come-lately made a hell of a racket to get in, waking everybody up. Can't we talk about something else?"

Tina smiled. "You might be interested to know I'm on the pill. That's why I was at the medical center, to get a prescription. I should be safe by the first of next week. Better still, I'm subletting Julie Everett's apartment for the summer. The rent is a steal at $150 a month. She wanted a reliable person to take care of her cat and her plants. The place is so full of plants, it reminds me of a green-house."

"Isn't Julie the one who has a king-size waterbed?" asked Tom with a gleam in his eye. "I can't wait to try it out."

"You sound more interested in the bed than in me," she complained.

"Thank God I've found you!" Pete van Pelt burst upon the scene out of breath and looking as if he'd just finished the Boston Marathon. Tom and Tina were jarred back to reality. "I thought you were going to be near the Anderson Bridge," he said.

"Originally Tina was going to meet me at the apartment. Instead I got a lift to Harvard Square. The boathouse was closer," said Tom.

"The police are in an uproar. Libertino wants to question you again. He has an order out for you to be brought in."

"I think it would be better if I showed up under my own steam," said Tom.

"Why do you think I've spent the past two hours tracking you down? Libertino's really gunning for you. Maybe you'd better find a lawyer."

Tom glanced at his watch. "One-thirty. I'll try Uncle Charlie at the Commander. For a corporate lawyer, he's had a lot of criminal law experience. It's amazing how many children of company executives get into trouble with the Chicago police."

Tina said, "Sue Bennet lives practically across the street in Dunster House. We can use her phone as well as get off the street." She pointed to a squad car barely visible in the distance, cruising down Memorial Drive.

Sue Bennet was packing to go home to Winnetka. She waved her hand toward the phone when Tina said, "Just a local call."

Tom got through to Charlie with no difficulty, filling him in on the death at the apartment. Tom said, "I tried to get you at the hotel early this morning after the police left. They have your name as one of the guests at the party."

"I got up early to go to Casner's lecture on estate planning for alumni. I think he scheduled it for 8:30 on purpose just to see how many of us would make it and manage to stay awake."

Tom said, "I won't beat about the bush. I've just heard the police have an order out to bring me in. I think I should go in voluntarily, but I'd like to talk to you first."

"Where are you calling from?"

"Dunster House, C entry, room 5."

"I'll be right over. Stay in the room and don't make any calls."

With the maze of one-way streets around Harvard Square and the certainty of heavy traffic on a Friday afternoon, Charlie knew he could make better time on foot than if he took a cab. There was no cab in sight, anyhow. Despite his concern about his nephew, passing through the Square brought back a flood of old memories. At this season Harvard Square was a melting pot of students, their relatives, alumni and the ever-present drug pushers, users, touts, pimps and townies. The faceless mass of humanity pouring into and out of the subway hadn't really changed in ten years.

When Charlie got to Dunster House, he asked to talk to Tom alone. Sue had finished her packing and was chatting with Tina and Pete.

Pete said, "My car's parked on a side street right off Memorial Drive. I'll be glad to drive you to the airport. Coming, Tina?"

"I'm staying right here to keep an eye on Tom," she said. Tom could hear the stubborn note in her voice and knew that any argument would be futile.

As Pete picked up Sue's bags to leave, Charlie said, "For God's sake, don't tell anyone where Endicott is. I need at least an hour with him before I deliver him to Libertino."

"Give us credit for some sense," said Pete. "When I leave the airport, I'll go back to the apartment and stay there until I hear from you. The police probably have someone watching the place."

"Are you sure they didn't follow you to the boathouse?" asked Charlie.

"I had Kevin drive me to the Coop. I ducked down into the subway there and came out another way, putting on a beret and dark glasses. You'd be surprised what they teach us now at Harvard. Then Kevin left my car on Flagg Steet near the Drive—a spot we'd picked out in advance—with the keys under the bumper in a magnetic box."

"I'd cut out the shenanigans, if I were you. You'll only convince the police you have something to hide, or worse still that you and Tom are in it together."

"Okay, okay," said Pete. "I'm off."

Charlie turned to his nephew. "Let's hear it from the beginning. The police must have found something to connect you with Fisher."

"He swore he wouldn't keep any records. I paid him in cash after each session. I never even told him my last name. From the way he acted, he thought 'Tom' was assumed."

"What kind of sessions?" asked Charlie.

"Tutoring, of course. I was scared to death my first year. I'd been at the top of my class at Brown. Here I barely passed Criminal Law, the only one-term course

I took the first term. The problem with this place is that you really don't know whether you're going to make it until you get the results of the May exams."

"We had the same worries when I was here as a student," said Charlie. "It's nothing to be ashamed of."

Tina put in her oar. "Now I understand why you completely neglected me last year. I'd been expecting great things after that first date in February."

"I got my grade on the exam the next day," said Tom, making a face.

Charlie said, "Save your romantic reminiscences for later, children. Our main job now is to coach Tom so that he tells a straight story, a believable story, and stays out of jail. I know something of this lawyer Fisher by reputation. He was a real hotshot lawyer until the IRS caught up with him. There are rumors he has resorted to blackmail in the past. A student sensitive about the fact he was being tutored might be a blackmail target."

"I don't know how he could have found out my last name," said Tom. "I never met him any place except at his apartment. I never wrote him. I never gave him a check."

"Did you ever give him your phone number?" asked Charlie.

"How would that help without a name or address?"

"There's a way to get the listing if you have the number."

"I don't remember giving him my number, but it's a possibility," said Tom.

"What if he wanted to cancel a tutoring session?" asked Charlie.

"He insisted that I call just before I came over to avoid that problem," said Tom.

"There are many other ways he could have discovered your name if he really wanted to. When I was a student here, many of the profs had seating charts with names and pictures. All Fisher needed was access to a chart in a required first-year course—buy a secretary a couple of drinks. Or he might have seen you in the Square with someone he knew—a casual question and he has the answer."

Tina said, "What it comes down to is your stupid pride. You didn't want anyone to know about the tutoring, especially me."

"Don't knock the tutoring," said Tom. "If I'd spent the time with you instead, I might not be here this year. I know I need my head examined. Still, I thought there was zero risk in lying to Libertino. I'd probably do it again in the same circumstances, but I'd never kill anyone to keep that kind of a secret."

"Had Fisher ever tried to put the squeeze on you?" asked Charlie.

"Never. Until he showed up at our party, I hadn't seen him for over a year when he criticized a practice exam. I'd have told him to go to hell if he tried anything."

"Were you surprised to see him at the party?" asked Charlie.

"Yes, but I thought it was just a coincidence. All kinds of weirdos tend to drop in when we're giving a party. I didn't think he had any sinister motive. We politely ignored each other which was easy to do in that mob scene."

Tina could not resist making a comment. "Sooner or later everyone in Cambridge turns up at Tom's apartment—or maybe it just seems that way. There's something familiar about Fisher I've been trying to remember. Wait a minute. I've got it. I've seen him with Emily Quince. They had something going."

"Who's Emily Quince?" asked Tom and Charlie, almost in unison.

"She has the apartment next to Julie Everett's, the one I'm subleasing for the summer. Every time I've been over to see Julie, Emily has dropped in to borrow or return something. She's a secretary, works for a law school professor."

"Now the name rings a bell," said Tom. "She's Rosie's secretary."

"You students actually call him 'Rosie'?" asked Charlie in surprise.

"Hell, he hadn't been here a week before we started, except in class of course. Someone asked him to a student party the first night he was here. Sometime after midnight he helped one of his crocked colleagues home and came back for three more hours of singing and boozing with the best of us."

Charlie raised a hand to stop him. "I'm sorry we got off the point. Let's work out our strategy for the meeting with Libertino. Think before you answer any question that goes beyond the obvious. That way I'll have time to stop you, if the question is improper or so tough that you ought to duck it for the time being. If I don't butt in, answer the question truthfully without volunteering any information. If he asks what we talked about this afternoon, tell him."

Tom asked, "Are you sure you should come with me? Would I have a lawyer with me unless I'm in a real jam?"

"You are," said Charlie. "You've lied to the police. Besides, who knows what they've turned up in Fisher's apartment. They must have some lead that points to you. Libertino may already be determined to book you. The only question in my mind is whether you should have a real criminal lawyer rather than an amateur like me."

Tom looked even more like death warmed over. "How do we get to the police station?"

"Is it still on Western Avenue near Central Square?"

"Yes."

"We could go by subway, but that's risky. I suggest that you call Libertino. Tell him you're coming in and will be there within half an hour. If he offers to have you picked up, say thanks but no thanks. We'll go by cab. Neither of us wants to be seen riding around Cambridge in a squad car."

CHAPTER 4

▼

Joe Libertino was in a bad mood. The interrogation room was too small, and the air circulation was terrible. The chief claimed he should question suspects one at a time, a good rule most of the time. Now he had this smart-aleck law student, Endicott, and his smart aleck lawyer uncle. The view from the lone window did nothing to improve the atmosphere—a run-down apartment building with three lines of tattered washing hanging from lines on sagging back porches.

"When did you find out we were looking for you?" Libertino asked Tom.

"About two hours ago."

"We talked to your buddy van Pelt about eleven this morning right after we'd searched Fisher's apartment. I figured it wouldn't take van Pelt long to find you if I had a man following him, a good man. He lost him at Harvard Square, almost like your buddy knew he had a tail and was trying to shake him."

"Pete didn't know where I was," said Tom, telling the literal truth. "He said it took him two hours to find me."

"Why didn't you come in right away?" asked Libertino.

"I wanted to talk to my uncle."

"Because you had a guilty conscience?"

"Only about lying to you. I did know Fisher. He tutored me in my first-year courses. I didn't want my friends to know. I had absolutely nothing to do with his death. I hadn't seen him for over a year when he showed up at our party last night."

"Maybe you felt strongly enough about keeping the tutoring a secret to shut him up for good."

"Look, Sergeant, the tutoring was over a year ago. Fisher had never threatened to tell anyone. In fact, he lived up to his reputation of being discreet. He made good money from tutoring. Why should he spoil business by shooting his mouth off?"

"His records do show a healthy business." said Libertino, picking up a ledger and passing it to Tom. "Do you recognize any of those names?"

Tom leafed through the ledger. The entries showed the ledger had been started three years ago. In three columns appeared dates, names and dollar amounts, these last usually being $25 or $50. He flipped to 1969, his first year as a law student. His name appeared frequently throughout the second term. He scanned the rest of the book. "There are only a few names I don't know. My guess is they're all law students. After all, there are other law schools in the area. Some of the names are surprising—John Rogers, for example. He turned down law review."

"Why?" asked Libertino.

"He's helping to support three younger brothers. John has a weekend job doing legal research for a Boston law firm. Every weekday night he does an hour and a half stint as a disc jockey. Law Review would take at least twenty hours a week. This way he gets paid for it."

"That Boston firm will probably offer him a full-time job when he graduates," threw in Charlie. "They may even be more impressed that he turned down the honor rather than accepting it. This way they get to know him and his abilities first-hand.

Tom was looking more closely at the ledger pages covering the past month. "I don't understand these recent entries for Rogers. As soon as he got his first year grades, he'd know that he didn't need any more tutoring."

Charlie Witherspoon looked over his shoulder. "The amounts are in a different column from the other entries. Maybe they're payments to Rogers for tutoring. From the volume of business Fisher was doing, he could have used some help."

"That checks with what Rogers told me," said Libertino. "Did you know he had another side line?"

"No, but it doesn't surprise me," said Tom. "He's one of the busiest guys I know; I've rarely seen him doing anything just for fun. There's almost always a bridge or poker game going on somewhere in our duplex. The players change, but I've never known Rogers to sit in."

Libertino said, "He claims he really got stoned at your party last night. He has only a vague recollection of being put to bed by someone. Was it you?"

"Yes," Tom said. "When I left him he was lying flat on his back completely out, with a foolish smile on his face, his arms folded on his chest, and his hands in a position to hold something. I'd have given him an Easter lily if I'd had one."

Libertino said, "I went to see him this morning at 11:30, after I'd been to Fisher's apartment and couldn't find you. His buddies had to hold him under a cold shower and pour two cups of black coffee down him before he was halfway awake. Do you think he was faking it last night?"

"Sergeant, have you ever tried drinking to all of the Newtons? If Rogers was faking it, he deserves an Oscar. He was just like a sack of potatoes when I was helping him home. He almost fell down the stairs, pulling me after him. He weighs over 200 pounds. I'm only 140. It would have been a disaster if he'd landed on top of me."

Libertino said, "Look at one other thing we found in Fisher's apartment, tucked into his bottom desk drawer.

1. +	5. -	9. +	13. +	17. -
2. +	6. -	10. +	14. -	18. +
3. -	7. -	11. +	15. +	19. +
4. +	8. -	12. -	16. -	20. -

Charlie said, "It looks like the answers to a true-false test. I've never heard of such a thing at the law school. Why don't you check with the Dean's office? They may be able to help you. Another possibility is that Fisher had something going over at the college."

Tom said, "It may simply be a tutoring aid."

"Mr. Endicott, are you going to stay put for a while?" Libertino asked. "I was ready to book you this morning. Now I'm willing to give you the benefit of the doubt at least until I've checked out the other angles."

"I've got a summer job with a Boston law firm, starting Monday. My parents live in Weston, which is the only other place I'm likely to be this summer."

"You're not out of the woods yet," said Libertino. "Get out of here before I change my mind."

Charlie nudged Tom. They went quickly without either saying another word.

*   *   *   *

Libertino put the Fisher file to one side and picked up the file on the death of a fourteen-year old boy. According to the autopsy report the cause was an overdose of heroin. My God! he thought. The drug problem in Cambridge was going from bad to worse. The boy had syringe marks on both arms—already an habitual user. This time a friend had found him in a coma with the needle still in his arm. The report went on to say that the stuff was exceptionally good—no evidence of quinine or sugar, usually used to cut the drug at least once in the chain of its distribution.

Libertino picked up the phone to call Frank Thomas in Washington. He and Frank had served together in Vietnam. Thomas was now Deputy Director of the Bureau of Narcotics under the Treasury Department.

"Hello, Joe. What can I do for you?"

"Frank, you old horse thief, maybe the shoe is on the other foot. I've got a report on the death of a teenage kid, a classic case of heroin overdose. Somehow he got hold of some virtually pure stuff. I thought you'd like to know. There's nothing to suggest it wasn't an accident. We're planning to close the file here in Homicide. Who the supplier is and where the stuff came from are things I can't do much about."

"Until just recently, most of the heroin coming into this country was South American and not very high grade," said Frank. "Two weeks ago we had a tip on a Gloucester fishing boat and alerted the Coast Guard. They stopped the boat coming in and found the kind of stuff you described almost pure white. A larger boat got away in the fog. We think it was a mother ship operation with several smaller boats taking shipments in to different ports to spread the risk. Hell, in May there are many deserted beaches where they could unload the stuff without being seen."

Libertino said, "We figure the kid either stumbled on the stuff accidentally or was close to someone high up in the chain."

"Keep me posted, Joe. We need all the help we can get in this dirty business. The quantity of all drugs going in to the northeast is increasing rapidly. It looks like the operation is being run from Boston or Cambridge. So far we've picked up only a few of the little guys. My men in the field have been working with a Lieutenant what's-his-name in your department."

"Collins," said Libertino. "Do me a favor and don't let him know you learned the news about the kid from me or his nose will be out of joint. I'll fill him in as soon as I've hung up and he can pass the news along through proper channels. Give me a call the next time you're in town. I'll buy you a lobster dinner."

Libertino went across the hall to the corner office where Lt. Collins sat in comparative splendor. The door was half-open, and he was alone. Bill Collins at forty-five had more than the beginnings of a beer belly and a barrel chest to go with it. With his crew cut and pug nose he looked like a caricature of a nazi officer from a war movie. Libertino laid the autopsy report on Collins' desk.

"We're about to close the file on this as an accidental death, but I thought you'd be interested. Heroin OD. Apparently uncut stuff of very high quality."

Collins glanced at the report. "The kid's name was Gomez, eh? Maybe it's only a coincidence, but we picked up a Pedro Gomez yesterday, selling heroin near the subway station at Harvard Square. We got the word from one of the undercover men the feds have here. The narc says this Gomez character is a real amateur. It was like he was walking around with a sign around his neck saying 'Horse for sale'. We let him be most of the day hoping he'd run out and lead us to someone more important."

"What happened?" asked Libertino.

"Schultz and O'Hara decided Gomez was no professional and were about to run him in when the suspect leaves the square to find his car, a beat-up VW bee-tle with the fenders practically falling off. They arrested him just as he opened the hood and was getting out more supplies. He had fifteen or twenty one-ounce packages, crudely made up with heavy duty aluminum foil and a professional looking five-pound sack. We don't have the lab report yet, but it sure looked like the real stuff—the same kind your kid Gomez died of. It could have been diluted at least four to one and sold onthe street for forty dollars an ounce. That's nearly $13,000 for the five-pound package, and he had at least two of those."

"How old is this Pedro Gomez?' asked Libertino.

"Twenty, according to his driver's license. No way any dealer would trust the kid with that quantity of first-rate, uncut horse."

"How does he say he got it?"

"Claims to have found two packages in a vacant lot."

"More likely he stole a car and found the packages locked in the trunk. These kids learn to use a jimmy before they're weaned."

"I think this kid is scared, Joe. If he had any connection with the mob, he'd have called a shyster and have been out of here by now. Instead, he hasn't even made one phone call. I think he wants to stay locked up as long as possible."

"Probably Miguel was a younger brother or cousin," said Libertino. "He may have been with Pedro when he latched on to the stuff."

"We still have Pedro in a cell if you want to talk to him. I don't see why he shouldn't admit he was Miguel's source. Nothing can hurt Miguel now. Pedro we've already got on five counts of distribution. It's a ripe case for plea bargaining."

CHAPTER 5

▼

Charlie Witherspoon had delivered Tom to an anxious Tina and joined Rosie at Chancery Club for the Class of 1960's cocktail party. They were five years older than the average age of the class, Charlie because of his over-education at other branches of Harvard, Rosie because he had been five years into a teaching career at a public high school when he decided to go to law school. Rosie had never regretted his superior knowledge of American history.

Charlie said, "Do you remember Bob Fleming's wife, June, who posed for an oil painting in nothing but a wig and a judge's robe—wide open at the front?"

"Do I!" said Rosie. "That babe was really stacked. The best part was when Fleming got into Austin West ten minutes ahead of the third-year tax class and substituted the nude for the picture of Lord Mansfield hanging on the wall behind the podium. Some wag made up a silly verse:

"Mansfield, Mansfield on the wall
Who is barest of us all?
Sally Rand is bare, 'tis true,
But barer far than she are you!"

"I was there, you bonehead! Professor Andrews didn't notice the nude painting behind him. He was too wrapped up in explaining a complex C-type reorganization. The class gradually caught on, but it was several minutes before laughter and the pointing caused Andrews to turn around. It broke him up, too."

After the second drink, Rosie drew Charlie off to one side. "I've got a problem I'd like to discuss with you. This afternoon my third-year students took my exam in evidence. This morning, three hours before the exam, I had an anonymous phone call, implying that someone had been able to get access to the exam and that there would be widespread cheating. My security on exams has always been very tight, so I ignored the call as a prank. After the exam one of my better students stopped by my office to see me. He, too, thinks there was cheating going on. I say, 'too' because I'm sure he was not the anonymous caller. It just wouldn't be in character for him, and the voice was entirely different."

Charlie said, "I don't understand. I thought there was a special exam program going on because of Cambodia and the student unrest. A student could either take the exam at the assigned place and hour or take the questions away with him, time himself, and turn in his answers any time up to two weeks later."

"In most courses, yes; in mine, no. I felt I had so much ground to cover I made up the exam in two parts, essay and true-false. I thought having the true-false questions out for two weeks would be too much temptation."

Charlie asked, "Did the true-false part by any chance have twenty questions?"

"How could you have known unless you ran into one of my students after four o'clock today? I thought you spent the afternoon at the police station."

Charlie explained how the police had found a paper with pluses and minuses on it at Fisher's apartment. "Don't jump to conclusions, Rosie. It's sheer speculation that the marks on that paper were answers to a true-false test. Even if they are, why does it have to be your test? I recall the pattern was a random one, but I don't recall the exact sequence. Let me try to call Libertino. Would you remember the pattern if he read it to you?"

"Certainly. I've got a copy of the answers in my pocket, the only one in existence I might add."

Charlie came back from the phone frustrated. "Libertino has been called out on a fresh homicide. I left word for him to call you at your office in the morning, assuming that you're going to put in a Saturday appearance."

"I'll either be there or in the Dean's office," said Rosie.

"Why did your student suspect cheating?"

"He was in the men's room in Langdell basement right after the exam. He heard two other students talking. They were furious because the word was out that the answers were on sale for 500 dollars. Turne—that's the student who came to see me—was sitting on the crapper in one of the stalls. When he came out, the other students were gone. He claims he didn't recognize their voices."

"Or didn't want to get involved," said Charlie. "I gather he didn't exactly chase after them. It would be tough to turn in a student in his third year, which is what those two might have to do. Anyone involved in the cheating would be booted out on his ear, and would stand a fat chance of getting into another law school of any standing."

"It's a large class," said Rosie. "He could be telling the truth."

"Anything else?" asked Charlie.

"I graded the true-false parts of the exam by machine before dinner. No one got a perfect score, but statistically there were too many papers with only one or two mistakes. They were tough questions, if I do say so myself. I'll know better when I grade the essay parts. I'm willing to bet that some of the high-scorers on the true-false questions won't do as well there."

"What are you going to do?" asked Charlie.

"It's a real mess. Graduation is too close. There's no practical way to give a substitute exam."

"You could throw out the true-false part."

"That's one solution," said Rosie. "It's a windfall to someone who messed up that part and unfair to the honest student who did well on it. I'll discuss the problem with the Dean in the morning. If Libertino's paper has the same answers, I'll be convinced that we have to do something."

"What exactly are your security precautions in getting examination questions printed?"

"My secretary delivers the questions personally to the printer. From the printer they usually go by special messenger to a safe in the administration building for distribution on the day of the exam. This time we were running late. I picked them up myself at the printer's to take them over to Langdell North where the exam was given."

"What about the answers to the true-false part?"

"I've told you; there's only one copy. Maybe I should call it a handwritten original. I've kept it in my wallet since I made the questions up."

Charlie speculated, "This Lawrence Fisher, the man who was killed last night, is supposed to have been a brilliant trial lawyer before he was disbarred. If he somehow managed to get hold of the questions, couldn't he have worked out the answers?"

"Yes, I suppose it's possible," said Rosie, grudgingly.

"How could Fisher get access to the exam?" asked Charlie.

"There are only two possibilities—one involves the printers, the other my secretary, Emily Quince. She delivered the copy to the printers and helped me proofread. She just isn't the type. Anyway, I refuse to think about it until I'm sure that the exam was stolen."

"Just one more question," said Charlie. "Did both parts of the exam go to the printers at the same time?"

"No, I took over the essay part myself three days earlier. I see what you're driving at. If someone is going to steal the exam, why not steal both parts. Of course, it would be practically impossible to detect cheating on the essay part. We could check the student's grade on the essay part against his general average, but early access to the exam questions would probably improve the student's grade only a few points."

Charlie frowned. "If Fisher had early access to the essay part questions, he could prepare different sets of good to excellent answers, paraphrased so that it would be hard to prove they came from the same source."

"There really wasn't enough time," said Rosie. "We were behind schedule as it was. Besides in a third-year course it would be suspicious if a student suddenly got a much better grade on an essay exam."

Charlie decided to call it a night. "After you talk to Libertino in the morning, let me know where things stand." He suddenly remembered why the name "Emily Quince" rang a bell, but he saw no reason to add to Rosie's problems prematurely.

On the way out Charlie stopped briefly in the library off the dining room on the first floor. Several law students were relaxing listening to classical music on an FM station. Charlie recognized the haunting strains of a Chopin piece. The name was on the tip of his tongue; his mother used to play it. The pianist finished. The disc jockey began to speak, but some late-comers to the cocktail party came through the room; the noise they made drowned out most of what the disc jockey was saying. Charlie heard enough to recognize the voice of John Rogers, the third-year student who lived downstairs from his nephew, moonlighting to pay his way through law school.

Charlie felt guilty about deserting Rosie, but he'd had more than enough of the Fisher murder for one day. Also he felt a yen for Chinese food, which Rosie couldn't stand. He walked to Harvard Square before he found a cruising cab, jumped in and gave the driver a Chinatown address.

CHAPTER 6

▼

Joe Libertino and his wife, Gina, lived in a one-bedroom apartment on Harvard Street, roughly half way between Harvard Square and Central Square. They had agreed to put off having children for the first five years of their marriage, conveniently ignoring the church rules about birth control. Gina had been out of the country for a week—a fact that had driven Joe up the wall. He was a lousy cook, worse at keeping the house clean, and he missed her terribly. He had been planning to meet her at the airport until this latest homicide had come up. Now, hours later, as Joe dragged himself up the front steps at five in the morning, he felt like a limp dishrag. The scratchiness in his throat and intermittent cough warned him to expect the granddaddy of all colds. Hell! The cough could be explained by the two packs of cigarettes he'd smoked that day. The crusher was that he had to be back at headquarters at nine for a meeting with Bill Collins.

The light was on in the bedroom. Joe opened the door to look in. Gina lay fast asleep with an open book beside her on the bed. With her dark hair, olive skin, high cheekbones and generous superstructure, she was a slightly lopsided version of Sophia Loren at her best. The lack of symmetry was only in the face and made it more interesting to Joe. He knew he was very lucky. He picked up the book, pulled up the covers very carefully, and turned off the light. From the cupboard outside the bathroom he grabbed a blanket and a pillow. In the medicine chest in the bathroom he found aspirin and Vitamin C. He stopped briefly in the kitchen to take his pills with a glass of water. When he got to the living room, he set the alarm for eight, took off only his shoes, and stretched out on the sofa with the blanket over him.

It seemed like minutes later when the alarm went off. He plugged in the coffee and went into the bathroom. The mirror told him he needed a shave; he knew he didn't have time for a shower. He didn't hear Gina go by the bathroom door, yet by the time he was rinsing off the lather he could smell bacon frying in the kitchen. One glance at his trousers told him they wouldn't do. He shouldn't have slept in them. They were due for a cleaning anyway. By the time he got into his gray flannels and a sport coat he felt almost human. Even the scratchiness in his throat had disappeared. He put a fresh pack of cigarettes in his jacket pocket, resisting the temptation to light one up before he drank his first cup of black coffee. He walked into the kitchen to find Gina scrambling eggs, with real coffee dripping through a ceramic pot instead of the instant coffee he'd been planning on.

"Honey," he said, "I thought I was being quiet. What got you up so early?"

"Just frustration, I guess. I got off the plane yesterday expecting you to meet me at the airport—no such luck." Gina was an assistant buyer for Filene's and had just returned from an expedition to Italy—her first solo venture—to buy leather goods in Milan and Rome. "I cook a special meal for you—*Saltimbocca alla Romana*, your favorite—and you call up saying you'll be late for dinner. At ten I put your dinner back in the oven to keep it warm. At eleven I turned the oven off. At midnight I went to bed hoping for better things, and fell asleep alone. My mother warned me never to marry a policeman."

Despite the controlled iciness of her voice, her eyes and a quiver at the corners of her mouth gave her away. He kissed her and hugged her until they both had to come up for air.

"I don't suppose you have time to make up for last night?" she asked. "No, you wouldn't have set the alarm and skipped your shower. Sit down and eat a decent breakfast at least. I knew you were going to try to sneak out of here with only black coffee."

"Cara mia!" Joe said. "I promise to be home for dinner tonight. Something came up just as I was leaving last night, a gangland slaying, body locked in the trunk of a car."

"Why couldn't someone else have handled it?" Gina asked.

"We're short-handed with Shaughnessy in the hospital. Besides, I've promised the chief that from now on I'll personally investigate any drug-connected homicide."

"How do you know there's a drug angle this time?"

"We found fifty ounces of heroin behind a trick panel in the car trunk," said Joe, realizing the weakness in his answer but hoping she'd miss it.

"If you're not home by six o'clock, I'll have all the locks changed," said Gina in a tone of voice that showed she'd missed nothing.

*   *   *   *

Joe lit up a cigarette, but not until he was well out of the apartment and half-way up Harvard street toward Central Square. Gina had been nagging him to give up smoking. He might just as well; these damn filtered things had no taste to them. He longed for an old-fashioned Lucky Strike. He'd even have walked a mile for a Camel.

There were puddles here and there in the street. It must have rained during the night, but there was hardly a cloud in the sky now.

Bill Collins had another cup of black coffee waiting for him. "That was some trick you pulled on the Gomez kid yesterday, pretending there was someone here to post bail for him. Gomez was so scared we'd *make* him leave the station that he really opened up. I'm sure he thought he'd be gunned down or worse the moment he got out on the street."

"He could have been right, Bill. This heroin bunch turns nasty when someone tries to horn in. Pedro admitted he and his brother did a job on a black in front of South Station about a week ago at three in the morning. Pedro slugged him just hard enough to stun him; Miguel grabbed his attaché case, and they both ran around the corner where they had a car waiting. I think they had a third man driving the car. We'll probably never know. Maybe Pedro is just as scared of the third man—if there was one—as he is of the gang they stole the drug from."

"You think that confession would stand up in court?" Bill Collins sometimes used dubious methods himself in interrogating suspects. He was delighted to see Libertino on the spot for a change.

"Look, Bill. You said it yesterday. You've got Gomez cold on drug charges right here in your own territory. Why worry about a minor mugging in Boston? The odds are he'll never be booked for that offense," said Libertino.

"Tell me about last night," Collins said.

"It was a three-ring circus. An old geezer called in to report that blood was seeping out of the trunk of a purple Caddy. After he called in he keeled over from the shock. We found him in a pay phone booth near Porter Square and rushed him to the emergency room at Mount Auburn. When we got back to the purple Caddy, there were a couple of blacks trying to force the trunk. They got away in a souped-up Jag. We'd still have caught them if it hadn't been for a yellow cab driving the wrong way on one of those crazy one-way streets near Harvard

Square. The Jag hit the rear end of the cab spinning it sideways so that it blocked the narrow street. We were lucky to be able to stop in time. We left a man to guard the Caddy. He had the trunk open by the time we got back the second time. The wallet we found on the body contained a driver's license in the name of Abraham Lincoln Jones. What have you been able to dig up on him?"

"Records reports a string of a.k.a.'s. In the trade, he's known as 'Whitey' because he deals only in heroin and coke. Only one arrest, and that only for possession, several years back. They tried to get him on a distribution rap once. An eager beaver suburban cop stopped the Caddy for going through a red light and made Whitey open the trunk for a search. They found about ten ounces of horse. Whitey must have been almost through his deliveries. The appeals court threw out the conviction, not because of the quantity but because of the illegal search. Hell, even a suburban cop would know better today. Incidentally Joe, you been going to night law school What if some dude had actually appeared to post bond for Gomez yesterday. Could he have refused it?"

"Bill, the usual type of bail is a bond, signed both by the prisoner and a bondsman. If the prisoner refuses to sign, no way is the judge going to let him go. If the bondsman offered to put up cash, I don't know what the judge would do," said Libertino.

Collins said, "The description Gomez gave you of that nigger fits your Caddy corpse, doesn't it—five feet five, skin purple black, dressed to the nines in a dark shirt, light tie, light gabardine suit?"

Libertino didn't like the word "nigger" any better than he liked the word "wop," but he wasn't about to try to reform someone who outranked him. At least Collins didn't call him a "wop" to his face. He said, "The description is dead on. However, it could fit a lot of blacks in Boston or Cambridge."

"Does the killing fit any pattern?"

"Most of the earmarks of a gangland slaying—hands tied behind the back, ankles bound, and a gag in his mouth. The oddball thing was two shots were fired instead of one. I think Whitey felt the gun against his head and tried to avoid the first shot. It got him in the neck and caused most of the bleeding. The second shot, just behind the left ear, must have been the one that finished him. I think the M.E. will agree. Five will get you ten he bought it because he lost that attaché case to the Gomez brothers."

"Was he killed in Cambridge?"

"I doubt it. We found the car near Sears in Porter Square. We got the call about midnight, but God knows how long it had been there. There's a regular bus route along Mass. Avenue there and a fair amount of traffic until after midnight. My guess is that he was killed in some deserted spot—or possibly in a garage with a silenced gun; then the Caddy with the body in the trunk was driven to the spot where we found it. Looks like my case until I can prove he was killed in some other jurisdiction. Shit! If I could prove that, I'd have the case solved." Collins' grunt was one of dismissal.

Joe Libertino went to check his desk. As he entered his office, the phone rang.

"Sergeant Libertino, my name's Grabowski, Walenty Grabowski. I'm a neighbor of yours at the apartment." Joe remembered the name on the mailbox and saying hello to the guy in the hallway several times. Apartment 3B. He also remembered the guy had a shrew of a wife. The building walls weren't all that thick. Vera Grabowski's shrill voice was a familiar sound Joe had difficulty tuning out.

"What can I do for you, Mr. Grabowski?"

"My wife has been nagging me."

What else is new? thought Libertino. "Mine does, too. I can't smoke a cigarette without getting an hour lecture."

"I gotta different kinda problem. I saw a mugging about a week ago, and I've kept my trap shut about it, except to Vera. That was my big mistake."

"Where did you see this mugging?"

"In Boston. I was coming back from…"

"Mr. Grabowski," Joe interrupted, "if you saw a crime in Boston, why call the Cambridge police? Besides, I'm in Homicide, and a mugging isn't usually fatal."

"Sergeant, you're my neighbor. I know you're not going to make trouble for me just for the fun of it. I flew down to New York on the shuttle Friday morning to see my brother, who was in the hospital recovering from an operation. I planned to fly back Saturday afternoon, but had to take the train. Logan airport was socked in with a pea-souper. Would you believe that the six o'clock from Grand Central didn't get in to South Station until nearly three a.m.?"

Libertino's ears pricked up. "What day was this?"

"A week ago Saturday. That is, it should have been Saturday, but they didn't make it until Sunday morning. The engine broke down in New Haven; we finally got a replacement that broke down in Providence. It took them two hours to repair it. I'd have been better off taking a bus."

"Exactly where did the mugging take place?"

"I was coming out of the Summer street side of the station near Atlantic Avenue when I saw these two young punks hit this black over the head. One of them ran off with the case the black had been carrying. The other threatened me with a blackjack and a knife and took off around the corner after his partner. I was too scared to follow, and the black seemed to need help."

"You'd have been crazy to follow," said Libertino. Can you describe the punks?"

"I didn't see them too well or for too long. All I remember is medium height, leather jackets, dark hair."

"What about the victim?"

"I got a real good look at him. A little shorter than me—and I'm only five-seven—black as the ace of spades, and what I'd call a flashy dresser. He came to when I went over to see how he was. I wanted to call an ambulance and the police. He said it wasn't worth the trouble. I got the impression he was no stranger to the police and that they were the last people he wanted to see."

"What about the case he was carrying?" asked Libertino. "There might have been something valuable in it."

"He claimed the only thing in the case was the remains of his lunch. Just then a car pulled up with a black woman driving. He got in and the car burned some rubber accelerating."

"Did you notice the car?"

"How could I miss it? A great big purple Cadillac with vanity plates: ALJ."

Somebody up there must like me, thought Joe. "Mr. Grabowski, you'll never know how much you've helped us. You did the right thing in calling in. I think I can promise there'll be no trouble for you either from us or from the Boston police."

"Thank God! Maybe Vera will lay off me for a while?"

Joe had seen Bill Collins leaving his office while Grabowski had been on the phone. Otherwise he would have rushed across the hall to fill Collins in on this latest piece of the jigsaw puzzle. He felt a sense of accomplishment, two cases pretty well wound up. Gomez could be written off as an accidental overdose. Whitey Jones would have to stay open for a while, if only for show. Otherwise some nosey reporter from the Globe would complain that the police did nothing about gangland slayings. Joe himself took a practical approach. He wasn't going to let anyone get away with murder if he could help it no matter how much the victim deserved to be killed. Still, when organized crime did a job, it was usually done professionally. The gun would never be found. The witnesses, if any, would never come forward, or if they did, they'd be scared into changing their testimony at the trial. The pros could bump off somebody at noon in Harvard Square and get away with it. There was practically no chance they'd ever get hard evidence to put away Whitey's killer. He could much more usefully work on something like the Fisher murder.

Joe took a look at the telephone messages on his spike and the pile of paperwork left over from yesterday. Maybe he could get through the urgent stuff before noon and get home to Gina.

CHAPTER 7

▼

Rosie was a confirmed bachelor, yet he insisted on having enough space to entertain and to put up friends, and he needed a garden to putter in. Fortunately a friend who taught at M.I.T. was on a sabbatical, and his three-bedroom house on Goldenball Road in Weston was available, one of the few small houses in town. Housing was so expensive that only a few town employees, mostly those who had inherited their homes, could afford to live there. Rosie's friend had bought before the building of the turnpike extension and the scarcity of good housing within easy commuting distance of Boston had pushed prices out of sight. Rosie got a special rate on the year's rental because his friend knew there would be no children or animals—except Rosie's well-behaved cat, Tigger. The owner didn't need to worry about the rugs and the upholstery, and he could safely leave the silver service and the hi-fi along with an excellent selection of tapes and records. If the M.I.T. professor had seen the local paper that week, he have found an additional reason to be glad he had rented to Rosie. Three chemistry students had managed to rent a house on Concord road where they used the basement to make LSD in commercial quantities. They might have gotten away with it if they hadn't given a very noisy party. A neighbor complained, and one of the guests, leaving the party half-stoned, ploughed into a police cruiser at the driveway entrance.

That Saturday morning Rosie dragged himself out of bed early enough to eat a leisurely breakfast. He planned on catching the 8:52 train from Kendal Green to Boston. To be more accurate, Tigger had dragged him out of bed because she was hungry. A multi-colored Maine coon cat with six toes on her front paws, she sat on the kitchen table performing the paw trick, a stunt that never ceased to delight Rosie. He always poured a little extra coffee cream into the pitcher. The mouth of the pitcher was too narrow for her to get her tongue far enough in. As a very young kitten she had quickly discovered the answer to the problem—dip the paw and lick the cream off the paw.

When Rosie opened the back door to let the cat out, he could see that yesterday's great weather was holding. He'd ride his bike, resisting the temptation to drive his Beetle to the station. As he coasted down one of the hills on Church street, he marveled at the amount of open land in a town less than fifteen miles from Boston. There was no industry at all except for a stone quarrying and crushing operation on the left, just before he got to the railroad tracks, dating from a time before the town had established strict zoning. The residents of Weston all seemed cut from the same cloth, well-paid professionals and executives mostly between the ages of thirty-five and fifty. Radicals and left-wingers became stick-in-the-mud conservatives once they moved to this suburb, at least as far as local affairs were concerned. Once they were under the wire, they began to talk about ways of keeping undesirables out and otherwise preserving the essential character of the town, such as continuing the ban on apartments, low-cost housing, and sewers which might make either of the former feasible. A few well-meaning souls, including some of the clergy, tried to drum up support for housing for the elderly. The effort failed, some said because no one could figure out a legal way to restrict the housing to those whose grandfathers had been born in the town. Weston was such a bedroom town it earned the name of Sleepy Hollow. There was even a movement afoot to zone it, birdwise, exclusively for pheasants.

Rosie locked his bike to a telegraph pole—only two cars on a Saturday morning—just as the train came into sight from the northwest. The bike, an ancient three-speed Raleigh, probably wasn't worth stealing, but Rosie wasn't taking any chances. The train picked up speed slowly. Rosie chuckled as they passed the bridge for the old main line of the railroad which now went due west through Weston center only as far as Sudbury. The roadbed on that line was so bad that on some stretches the maximum speed was ten miles per hour. There was just one train a day each way on weekdays only. Only a small group of loyal commuters used the line. The Boston & Maine management claimed that it could buy each of them a Cadillac, close down the line and still save money. Some said the service would have been abandoned long ago if the B & M employee in charge of terminating service hadn't lived in Wayland, using the line to get to and from his office in North Station.

*   *   *   *

Twenty minutes later Rosie left the train at Porter Square in Cambridge, close to the spot where the purple Cadillac had been found with the body in the trunk. Rosie normally walked to his office at the Law School; today he was pressed for time. He hoped to hear from Sergeant Libertino about the true-false test. He wanted to spot-check the essay part of some of the exams of those students who had excelled in the true-false part. Then he had a ten o'clock meeting with the Dean to decide how to handle the mess. On a Saturday morning he might wait longer for a bus than it would take him to walk the entire distance. He started out walking, looking over his shoulder from time to time to see whether a bus was coming. It wouldn't do to be between bus stops when a bus came along. Some of the drivers took a perverse delight in starting up just in time to prevent a hurrying would-be passenger from catching the bus.

During the week Rosie took an earlier train if the weather was half-way decent. He loved to window shop in the variety of specialty shops that lined both sides of Massachusetts Avenue on his way, places that sold exotic foods, wicker-ware, secondhand books, handwoven fabrics, leather goods, and homemade ice cream, among other things. This morning Rosie was in luck. He spotted a bus coming just as he neared the second bus stop.

On his way into his office in the administration building he passed a sure sign of spring, the words, "Orpheus loves Eurydice," scrawled in yellow chalk on the red brick wall. This message was new to Rosie and welcome comic relief. Some of the old-timers remembered the same graffiti as far back as the thirties.

Rosie unlocked his office door, grateful that his secretary, Emily Quince, wasn't coming in today. She'd received a call from a hospital in New Hampshire and had hurried off to check on her sick father. It was just as well. He couldn't face the woman until he had more evidence, and he really didn't want to face her at all. Maybe the problem would go away. The phone rang.

"Good morning, I'm Sergeant Libertino, Homicide. I'm trying to reach Professor Rosenblatt."

"Speaking, Sergeant. My friend, Charles Witherspoon called you yesterday evening. He thought the piece of paper you found in Lawrence Fisher's apartment might possibly be connected with part of an examination in my evidence course."

"Right, professor," said Libertino. "I've got the paper right here." He read off the pluses and minuses.

Rosie took his list of answers from his pocket and compared it with what he had taken down over the phone. "Thank God!," he said. "They're not the same. Sorry to have bothered you, Sergeant."

Libertino signed off, saying, "Thanks, professor. Let me know if you hear of any other true-false test given recently."

Rosie hung up. Then he started to have second thoughts. He hadn't told the whole truth to Libertino. Fisher's list corresponded to the correct answers to his test for all but two questions. Fisher had been a brilliant student as well as a courtroom lawyer of ten years' experience. Still the questions were tough, and he might possibly have come up with two wrong answers. Rosie refused to consider the possibility that he, Rosie, could have made a mistake. That way lay madness that could trouble him with lingering doubts. He knew it was hard to design a true-false question that was not false in some aspect to a professional hairsplitter.

Another thought struck him. If Fisher sold a poor student all the right answers, the result would stick out like a sore thumb, the more so if he sold the same answers to several poor students. It would also be risky to have the cheaters miss the same questions. Possibly Fisher had sold several sets of answers each of which had one or two different wrong answers. The piece of paper found in Fisher's apartment might have been prepared in anticipation of a sale that fell through, perhaps an attack of conscience on the part of the student.

Rosie looked at his watch. Yesterday he had isolated the high scorers on the true-false part, concentrating on the fifteen students who had eighteen or nineteen correct answers. He sampled their answers to the essay questions. Most of them were reasonably good, excellent in spots. May be his sense of judgment was deserting him. Five papers were in a doubtful category—no better than low to middle C's on quick inspection. Even if further examination confirmed this estimate of the grades, he doubted there was enough evidence to justify expelling anyone. It was statistically unlikely for five C students to do that well, but anyone could get lucky on a true-false test even with the deterrent of having half the number of wrong answers subtracted from the number of right answers in scoring. It might help to check the grades of these students in other courses.

He looked at his watch again. It was time he got moving. It would never do to keep the Dean waiting.

The Dean listened to Rosie's account of the problem and suggested lie detector tests for the students, more as a trial balloon than a recommendation.

Rosie said, "So much depends on the skill of the polygraph operator and the physiology of the subject. Charlie Witherspoon, as classmate of mine here, told me about a Chicago warehouse employee who systematically stole from his employer over a period of two years. The night watchman even helped him load his station wagon believing the story that he was picking orders for emergency deliveries. This character passed a lie detector test with flying colors."

"And I've heard of innocent people who have guilty reactions when tested," said the Dean.

"It's no wonder that the courts have been generally reluctant to accept the results as evidence," continued Rosie. "I'd certainly hate to see a student's career ruined by such a test or his refusal to take one. I had another idea on the way over here. I'm not sure I like it any better than yours."

"Don't keep me in the dark," said the Dean.

"I could ask each student to explain his answers," said Rosie, "or perhaps to take the test again with the questions in a different order."

"If he failed either of those tests," said the Dean, "all you'd know is what you'd known all along—that he was either a lucky guesser or a cheater. I agree the evidence is inconclusive. It's too late to give a substitute exam even if you had one all prepared. Normally the third-year students would be through by now, but with the sit-in at the administration building and the fire at the printers the whole exam schedule has been fouled up. For the first time in history we let the students pick up the questions and take the exams on their own. Now this happens, the possibility of cheating during a proctored exam."

"It hasn't been an easy year for any of us," said Rosie. "You've had the worst of it with all the student unrest. I think the best answer to my problem is to throw out the true-false results and grade on the essay part only."

"I agree, Rosie. It's the best solution to a nasty problem, but there's one more essential point to consider. I don't want either of us, or the law school we represent, to be in the position of obstructing justice. We've an obligation to explain this mess more fully to the police in case they want to question any of your students. There are only a few more days before they disappear. If there's any evidence to connect any of your five students with the death of Lawrence Fisher, we'll have to take another look at the cheating question. I can understand how a third-year student might kill to prevent a disclosure that he had cheated, a disclosure that would end a career before it began."

"Let me try out an idea on you," said Rosie. "This Charles Witherspoon I mentioned is here in Cambridge for his tenth reunion. He's worked with the Chicago police on several murder cases. He has a good practical knowledge of criminal law and police procedure, unusual for a corporate lawyer. If his law firm can spare him, maybe we can persuade him to stay on for a few days. With Sgt.

Libertino's consent, Charlie could participate in the questioning and protect both the students and the law school."

"If he'll volunteer, I'd be delighted. My budget for legal expense is sadly depleted."

Rosie looked at the clock on the Dean's desk. His watch had stopped for the third time that week. "I'll try to get Libertino first. Charlie's expecting to hear from me before noon. He knew I'd be talking to the sergeant this morning."

The Dean said, "Why don't you ask Witherspoon to join us for lunch. I'll arrange for a private room at the faculty club or else a table in the corner where we can have some privacy. The place should be practically deserted today, anyway. We can decide at lunch exactly what role Witherspoon should play. One thing I'm sure of." He turned to glare at Rosie. "As long as I'm dean here there won't be another true-false test given at this law school."

*   *   *   *

Rosie called Libertino, getting him just as he was leaving. "Sergeant, there may be some connection after all between my true-false test and the paper you found in Fisher's apartment." He explained about the five students with erratic performance on the different parts of his exam and the logic of his answers and Fisher's being slightly different.

"Professor, if I hadn't been really zonked from loss of sleep this morning, I'd have demanded to see your true-false answers so that I could make my own comparison. How long will these five students be around?"

"Until late Wednesday afternoon at least. They're all taking a course with a final being given then."

"Can you meet me here at headquarters about ten?" asked Libertino. "I've got to go home now and get some sleep."

"May I bring Charles Witherspoon with me? You'll remember him as Tom Endicott's uncle. The Dean would like him to represent the Law School in this matter."

"Sure. I'm not committing myself to let him sit in on the questioning of the students. We can talk about that tomorrow."

CHAPTER 8

▼

Barney's Bookstore was a Cambridge institution. Located on Mass. Ave between Harvard and Porter Squares, it had been a Mom and Pop grocery in the thirties, with a small apartment upstairs for the owners. Barney and his wife bought the place in 1939 and turned it into a bookstore specializing in second-hand textbooks. In the forties and fifties, business flourished as the number of students in a twenty-five-mile radius grew by leaps and bounds. Gradually the market for secondhand textbooks dwindled. Somehow the authors managed to get out new editions with just enough changes in the page numbers to prevent a student with the old edition from following the assignments. Also the Xerox machine made possible jerry-built textbooks, 8-1/2" x 11" copies stapled together. Barney couldn't keep up with these developments. He didn't want to make the capital investment required to handle new books

When Dapper Dan Callahan bought out Barney's widow in 1965, he found a typical secondhand bookstore. Signs in neat hand lettering divided the inventory by category. There was unbelievable diversity, even a section with popular sheet music from the thirties and bound classical piano music. The paperbacks hadn't been tended to in years. Everything was in a complete jumble. Callahan spent the better part of two weeks sorting things out and buying new stock so that the store would appeal to a wider clientele.

Dapper Dan, a wiry type just under six feet, still had all of his hair—chestnut curls that women longed to run their fingers through, and sometimes did. He'd retired from a local private school at fifty-five, misjudged his ability to live on a meager pension, and was forced to go back to work.

On this particular Saturday morning, Lt. Bill Collins was the only customer in the store, not surprising because the great exodus of students was well under way. Collins was in the stacks behind the checkout counter looking for a Mickey Spillane or a Zane Grey western, when he heard a voice he was sure he knew.

"Do you have a book about Chopin?" He made the word sound like cutting wood. Collins peered around the corner managing to stay hidden in the shadows. Yes, it was Tony Scarlotti, a swarthy Mediterranean type, barrel-chested, slung low to the ground, and weighing in at 200 pounds. He'd been arrested several times on drug charges, but not recently. They'd never been able to make any of the charges stick. Witnesses had a way of disappearing or changing their minds. They called him "Tony the Scar" partly because of his name and partly because of a curved welt on his cheek, made by a member of a rival gang who'd wound up in cement boots in the harbor.

Dapper Dan Callahan spoke up, keeping a perfectly straight face, "You mean the composer, Frederic Chopin?"

"Yeah, he wrote some ballads my wife is crazy about." He reached into his jacket pocket to pull out an envelope just far enough for it to be seen.

Callahan didn't react except to point. "Over there is a section with books about music and musicians. I don't recall any biography of Chopin in stock, but you can look. There is a four-volume encyclopedia that is certain to have three or four pages on him—right there on the bottom shelf. You're welcome to browse through it. Of course, I'd be glad to order something for you. The best-known biography is by Ludwig, I believe."

Scarlotti went across to the music section and went through the motions of looking at the titles; it was clear that his heart wasn't in it. He picked up Volume I of the encyclopedia and flipped through it perfunctorily. Then he left the shop, trying unsuccessfully to look casual about the whole encounter.

Collins was again the only customer in the shop. He came out where Callahan could see him. They were on friendly terms because of many previous visits."Mr. Callahan, I'm a police officer," he said, taking out his wallet to show identification.

"I remember your telling me that when we were talking about the realism—or lack of it—in detective fiction."

"That man who just left is a suspected criminal. I doubt that he has much interest in music, particularly classical music."

"I'd go along with that, judging from his pronunciation of 'Chopin'," said Callahan, who had minored in music at Oberlin.

"Tell me, has he ever been in your place before?"

"He was in here one Saturday several weeks ago. I was tied up on the phone when he came into the store, so my assistant waited on him. I didn't hear anything except the tail end of their conversation—t wasn't memorable. You remember Jim Walters, don't you, the guy who looked like a human string bean.?"

"Yeah, sure I do," said Collins. "Where is he today?"

"Once the students go, I don't need an assistant. During the school year it's different. Even though I don't handle textbooks the students come in looking for escape fiction."

"Have you got an address for Walters?"

Callahan opened a filing cabinet and pored through some papers. "15 Hastings Hall, Cambridge 38. He was a law student. Not that the address will do you much good. He said he was going back to California."

"Between you and I, Callahan, I think we got too many lawyers already. Please let me know if any more strange types come in asking about musicians. Here's my card. For God's sake, don't mention this to nobody."

Collins paid for two paperbacks he had picked up, left the store and hurried to his car parked nearby. As head of narcotics control he rated a two-way radio in his personal car, a three-year old Peugeot. "Headquarters, Collins here. Is the camera truck free?"

"Just a minute, Lieutenant, I'll check."

Collins saw Callahan come out on the sidewalk briefly, then go back into his store.

"It's all gassed up and ready to go," said the cop on the radio. "Where do you want it?"

"Send it with the usual crew to Barney's Bookstore, on Massachusetts Ave. between Harvard and Porter Squares. It's on the west side—big sign—you can't miss it. I want a picture of everyone who goes in or out until their nine p.m. closing."

Collins kept his eye on the door for the next ten minutes until a panel truck pulled up and parked across the street. The sign on the truck said, "Ajax Television—We fix it either at your place or ours—Repairs guaranteed for ninety days." The two men inside were dressed in overalls and looked like the real thing.

CHAPTER 9

▼

Tina Forbes had gone home to Scarsdale for the weekend. Her parents, long on the brink of divorce, were having another crisis. Both of them urged her to come, even if only for two days. She hated being caught in the middle and didn't think the visit would do any good, but she felt obligated to make the effort. At least she'd been able to move her stuff into Julie's apartment—with Tom's help—before she caught the plane to the White Plains airport Friday night. Her summer job started in Boston Monday morning; Tom was coming to dinner that evening.

Tom, at loose ends with Tina gone, went to the movies with Pete van Pelt. The Harvard Square theater was holding over the Bogie films another week. They were always popular during exams. Tonight it was "Casablanca," Tom's favorite. The counterpoint of *La Marseillaise* and *Die Wacht am Rhein* was a beautiful four-Kleenex bit. There wasn't a dry eye in the theater. After the movie they decided to walk back to Central Square on Harvard street. It had been raining hard earlier; now the moon and the stars were out, and the smell of late spring flowers hung in the air.

"There's a party over at the med school," said Pete. "Herb Freeman told me to bring anyone I liked, even you."

"No thanks, Pete. The last time I went to one of his parties I was dehydrated for a week. He dished out something positively lethal called a Velvet Hammer. It turned out to be 100% ethyl alcohol—that's the same as 200 proof—and grape juice. It tasted very innocuous going down but gradually developed the kick of twenty mules. Besides, I'm still not out of the woods with the police over that

Fisher mess. I want to be able to think straight tomorrow in case the sergeant decides to ask me more questions."

They cut north on Dana street to Inman avenue, only half a block from their apartment. As they neared number 236, a car started up with its lights on high beam and roared past them. Tom turned to look at the license plate. It was so dirty he probably would not have been able to read the number even if the bright headlights hadn't affected his vision. A form on the sidewalk groaned, tried to get up and fell back. Tom and Pete ran the last few steps.

"It's John Rogers," said Tom. "Call the police for an ambulance and bring a blanket with you when you come back. It's beginning to get chilly." He took off his jacket, folding it to form a pillow that he placed under Rogers' head.

"What happened, John?"

"Beat up—strangers—hurts to talk."

"Don't try; it can wait until you're feeling better." Tom rode in the ambulance to Mount Auburn's emergency room, and waited around a half an hour until an intern came out to report.

"Your buddy's going to be fine, no internal injuries or permanent damage as far as we can tell, although I'll show the X-rays to the resident as soon as I can get hold of him. Rogers has had a thorough going over by professionals. I've seen the same sort of injuries before in a man who hasn't paid a loan shark on time, a first warning so to speak. He's a mass of bruises and will be sore for at least a week. We've given him a painkiller and a sedative and put him in the ward for the night. With luck he can go home tomorrow. Give me a call in the morning. My name's Phillips, Paul Phillips."

"You mean you'll still be on duty in the morning?" asked Tom incredulously.

"Lately, we've been on call for seventy-two hours at a time," said Phillips. "It's worse than usual because three interns are down with mononucleosis."

"How can you function without adequate sleep? I suppose if things are quiet you get to catnap now and then."

"The lucky patients catch me at the beginning of my shift," said Phillips, smiling.

Tom went from Mount Auburn to the Commander Hotel. It was on his way back to his apartment, and he was hoping to find his uncle in. His timing was perfect. Charlie was just picking up his key as Tom walked into the lobby.

"How was the banquet?" Tom asked.

"Much less fun than the cocktail party last night—too many pompous speeches."

"I've just come from the emergency room at the hospital. John Rogers has been beaten up."

"Good grief! Why don't you come up to the room where we can discuss it in private. I've got some Black Label. We can ring room service for ice and soda."

"If it's Black Label, forget the ice and soda. I'll manage with a little tap water."

When they got to the room, Tom said, "John wasn't well enough tonight to talk much. From what he was able to say on the way to the hospital the beating may be connected with his part-time job as a disc jockey. I'm going to call the intern in the morning to find out whether we can bring him home in Pete's car. Except for the fact that he was attacked right in front of our apartment where Fisher was killed, I can't think of any connection with the murder. It's possible the beating was meant for someone else. I felt that I just had to talk to somebody about it." Tom paused to catch his breath. "I don't know why I'm bothering you with all this when you're flying back to Chicago tomorrow."

"I was. The Dean has asked me to stay to help in an investigation relating to Fisher's death and some irregularities at the law school. You'll have to promise to keep what I'm going to tell you under your hat."

"If you're talking about the cheating on the evidence exam, the word is already out. At dinner last night I heard some students talking about it at the next table. One of them was very bitter, complained he spent much more time on the true-false part than he should have. Now the betting is they'll just throw out that part and stick everyone with his grades on the essay questions."

Charlie marveled at how well the grapevine still worked. Either there had been a leak or it was just a coincidence. The students could easily have come to the same conclusion that Rosie and the Dean had.

"Do you remember with pluses and minuses that the police found in Fisher's apartment?" asked Charlie.

"Yes, you were speculating yesterday that the signs might stand for the answers to a true-false quiz. I wondered last night when I heard Rosie had given such a test."

"The answers to Rosie's test tallied almost exactly with the signs on Fisher's paper. Fisher somehow got hold of at least some of the exam questions in advance."

"That guy really knew his law," said Tom. "I wish I could have seen him in action defending a client in court."

"How well do you know Emily Quince?" asked Charlie.

"I've never met her, but Tina keeps talking about her. Emily has become something of a legend. It's really a sad thing that she's the butt of so many jokes."

"How is that?"

"The story goes that five years ago she got engaged to Lawrence Fisher. He was in prison then for tax evasion. She went to see him every week for two years."

"Five years is a long time for an engagement," said Charlie.

"I can't imagine waiting that long," agreed Tom. "Maybe Fisher had everything he wanted without getting married. I've heard that some of the women students he tutored paid in services instead of cash."

"Has Tina said whether Fisher had any intention of marrying Emily?" asked Charlie.

"According to Julie Everett—this is double hearsay—Emily thought he was stalling. She kept deluding herself. She filled one hope chest and was well on her way to filling a second when Fisher was killed."

"It seems likely that Fisher got a copy of the true-false questions from Emily Quince," said Charlie. "Possibly without her knowledge. Rosie told me she delivered the questions to the printer. Fisher could have met her—seemingly by accident—made an excuse to stop somewhere, and taken a picture of the papers while she was powdering her nose."

"Sounds a bit far-fetched to me," said Tom. "These law school secretaries weren't born yesterday. I can't imagine her letting the papers out of her sight for a minute."

"She may have let her guard down because Fisher was her fiancé and not a student. Also, she may have been more careless because she didn't have the answers and the general laxity this year. After all, in every other course the students could pick up the questions and were on their own for a week." Charlie frowned as if he didn't really believe much of what he was saying.

"What's the alternative?" asked Tom.

"That she'd do anything Fisher wanted her to because she's a sex-starved spinster—that someone in the printshop was bribed—that the whole thing is merely a coincidence."

"Is it possible that Fisher got the questions, but the cheating question is unrelated to his death?" asked Tom.

"I think I see what you mean," said Charlie. "Fisher stole the questions from Emily, made up a set of the answers, but couldn't find any takers when he tried to sell them. It's possible, yet the older I get, the less I trust coincidences such as five mediocre students doing very well on just one part of an exam."

Tom said, "Even if some students cheated, Fisher's death may not be connected. Where do you go from here?"

"I'm meeting Sgt. Libertino and Rosie tomorrow at the police station to decide how to question the students. Libertino is checking Fisher's records to see if any of their five names appear. Someone who needed to be tutored would be a good candidate to buy exam answers."

"I'm glad I'm not one of those five students," said Tom. "The way the sergeant looked at me yesterday he was ready to lock me up and throw the key away."

"How likely is it that a student would cheat?" asked Charlie.

"Not likely at all, in my opinion," said Tom, "especially for a third-year student. The odds are about a hundred to one that he'll do well enough to graduate. Also, by the time he's taking his last finals, his career grade average is pretty well cast in concrete. Even a score of 80 (A+ in Harvard's weird grading system) on the true-false test would be too little and too late to make up for three years of mediocrity in other courses, not to mention the essay part of the evidence exam."

"That's just about what the Dean said to me at lunch. While I thought he was indulging in wishful thinking, you both may be right. Perhaps you should pursue a career in law school administration. Now tell me about John Rogers."

"There's not much to tell yet. His face is too sore for him to talk without pain."

"He was hardly coherent when I talked to him. I'm hoping we'll get more out of him tomorrow even if they have to keep him in the hospital longer for observation."

"What exactly did he say about his disc jockey job?" asked Charlie.

"The only words that made sense were 'That damned radio station.'"

Charlie said, "I heard the tail end of one of his announcements last night on the radio at Chancery Club—after some piano music. What he said sounded perfectly innocuous."

CHAPTER 10

▼

For Bill Collins, Sunday was usually a day of loafing with the paper, watching sports on television, and drinking beer. He counted on Mabel, his wife, to get the children to Sunday school and to do the churchgoing for both of them. He also expected Mabel to bring him beer and sandwiches from time to time so that he wouldn't have to leave his reclining chair except for calls of nature.

Today he was restless. He had called headquarters twice Saturday after leaving the book store once to make sure the TV film of the traffic at the store had been compared with their rogues gallery of known dealers and once to check on drug arrests for the day. He just couldn't believe that Tony the Scar would go into a place like Barney's unless something crooked was going on.

Finally he threw the sports section down in disgust. "Mabel, I'm going down to the station for about an hour. I should be back in time for the Red Sox game. How about having one of your Reuben sandwiches ready for me? I saw all the fixings in the ice box."

"That's what I was planning to give you," said the long-suffering Mabel.

At noon on a Sunday, Collins was lucky to find someone in the audio-visual section. There weren't enough qualified officers to run and maintain the sophisticated equipment on a round-the-clock basis seven days a week, although the need was frequently there. The contents of some of the tapes and films were so sensitive that the chief was reluctant to hire civilian technicians, even if there'd been enough money in his budget to do so. When the section was first started six months ago, it had only one full-time man. This proved impractical. Another was soon added so that one man could be out in the field while the other was back at the lab, maintaining the spare units and working on recorded tapes, both sound and video, to bring out critical features. Sometimes the audio sounded like Donald Duck and the video had too little contrast to enable the viewer to identify people and places.

Pete Sullivan's joining the police force had been a godsend. His older brother was an engineer with a local television station and knew all the tricks of the trade. Pete was a quick learner. His interest in cameras and electronics was so strong that after a full eight-hour shift walking a beat or as second man in a cruiser, he liked nothing better than to assist the regular man in the audio-visual lab. At first, of course, he was an unpaid volunteer. Later his knack of making garbled tapes intelligible and cleaning up the video made him invaluable. The chief found a way to pay him overtime rates in an emergency. Sullivan's "evidence" had already been the key factor in securing two convictions. He was wearing high-fidelity earphones and an intent look when Bill Collins came into the room.

Sullivan said, "I've got some bad news for you, Lieutenant. Gus Swenson is dead. The chief just called from the hospital."

"I'll get the bastid who did it if it's the last thing I do," said Collins.

"No, no, Bill. He had a heart attack in a bar last night. For a while they thought he was going to make it, but the heart muscle was damaged too much. He had a second and fatal attack in intensive care."

"Swenson was one of our best undercover men. He did like to keep things to himself, though, until he thought he knew all the answers. I know he was working last night—meeting someone who claimed to know how horse is being distributed around here. He wasn't ready to tell me who, and like a fool, I didn't push him."

"He came to see me Saturday afternoon," Sullivan said. "I gave him one of those new super-sensitive mikes to try out. The built-in transmitter has a range of over 200 feet. Usually, the truck can get close enough to monitor it. Unfortunately, Swenson wore the mike on his necktie covered up partially by a tie clasp."

"Damn!" said Collins. "I can guess what happened. Swenson and his smelly old pipe. God knows when he cleaned it last. Every time he drew in it made a terrible racket."

Sullivan nodded and smiled ruefully. "Sounds just like Niagara Falls on the tape. I remember reading about a CIA man who had a similar mike embedded in an olive at the bottom of an empty martini glass. It worked fine until he forgot where the mike was and ate the olive. Fortunately our tape may not be a total loss. I've been building my own noise filter from parts we have in stock here. It's all done except for two condensers which I can't pick up until Monday morning when the stores open."

"Have you tried Boston?" asked Collins.

"Natch. Their lab just happens to be out of the sizes I need."

"Keep me posted," said Collins. "The chief has really been on my back about the increase in drug traffic. The death of that young spic didn't help us with the local press, either. There were two bleeding hearts articles. What I really came in for was to see the video on Barney's Bookstore."

"They did some beautiful camera work there," Pete said. "In one shot of a subject's chin you can count the hairs on a mole if you want to blow it up a little. I did just for the hell of it when I was running the video tape for Fitzpatrick. He had a bunch of mug shots from Records with him and made me run through the tape twice."

"Shit on a shingle!" said Collins. "Fitz knows everyone in the trade in this neck of the woods—users too. I wonder why he bothered with the mug shots. Still, I'd like to see the video for myself."

Pete ran the beginning of the reel at normal speed, hoping in vain to catch Collins sleeping at the switch. The old pro had an elephant's memory for faces.

"Go back to the beginning," Collins said. "I want to see a close-up of the second or third guy to enter the store: the tall bugger wearing a beret, a silly grin, and an army field jacket. That's the one! There's something familiar about him. It's just the rig that's different. It's your fuckin' boss, Jack Boyle. He'd be a natural for undercover work. I hardly reccanized him."

Pete said, "I can't wait to see his face when he finds out he walked right into a stakeout. Let's pull him in for questioning."

"Monday's soon enough," said Collins, chuckling. "I'll give him a hard time. You can count on it."

*   *   *   *

An hour later Collins was ready to give up. His eyes were beginning to water; his stomach was growling for that sandwich and a couple of cans of beer. If he didn't get home soon, he'd miss the start of the ball game—those damn Yankees again. He was putting on his jacket to go when he remembered something that didn't fit.

"Pete, go back to an early part of the tape—you remember that blonde in the light gray coat with the loud scarf?"

"Sort of a Paisley print, right? I'll find it. I remember she dropped her purse. The camera zoomed in for a close-up just as she was picking it up."

"Freeze it right there," said Collins as the camera showed a spot right in front of the entrance to the store. "What's that mark on the sidewalk directly in front of the door?"

"Wait a minute. I'll blow it up for you on the monitor. It's a circle with two smaller circles inside, like Orphan Annie's eyes."

"Do you have the faintest idea what it is?"

"You're in luck," said Pete. "My wife is really into astrology. She keeps shoving these horoscopes under my nose. I was born on the fourth of July. They say my mother was scared by a firecracker. That sign is Cancer, the crab. They call it 'Moon children' now so people won't think of the disease."

"I'd swear it wasn't there when I went in the store yesterday morning. Some kids were playing catch and the ball rolled up to me on the sidewalk just in front of the door."

"Fran—that's my wife—claims the sign of the crab is used by some gypsy tribes to warn of disease or danger or simply to alert the tribe that the place is no good for a handout," said Pete. "She may have made it up; she's got a good imagination."

"That's it!" said Collins. "When that bastid Scarlotti left the store, he chalked the mark on the sidewalk as a warning."

"I don't understand," said Pete. "Wouldn't the camera have picked up anyone who got close enough to read the warning?"

"Remember how great the weather was yestiddy, and all those fancy little shops along that part of Mass. Ave.? The sidewalk was jammed with window shoppers, people just out for a walk, and cheapskates saving bus fare on their way to Harvard Square. We'd have needed ten cameras to get close-ups of everyone passing Barney's. The guys we want are probably trained to walk by the drop point and give the place the onceover—they keep walking if they see that crab. When Fitz comes in Monday, I'll have him take another look at the video. Even without a close-up he might recognize someone who was passing by. Sometimes the way a person walks is as good as a fingerprint, better than a photograph."

"Poor Fitz," said Pete. "He had a theory that any pusher would pick up his stuff inside the store and go out the back way as a security measure. He made up a chart and checked off the people who came out against those who went in."

"That Fitz is a thorough sunnava bitch," said Collins, "but that theory won't fly. The only other door is an emergency fire exit. When it's opened, it sets off an alarm. More often than not Callahan's there by himself. He'd lose his shirt if any customer could pick up a stack of books and sneak out the back way."

"What about Callahan himself?" asked Pete. "A bookstore is a natural for a drug distribution point. A lot of the business, the second-hand books part, is strictly cash. No reason for the customer to identify himself."

"That's true," said Collins, "but the owner of the store wouldn't have to be mixed up in the racket. Anybody could come in and browse for hours without causing suspicion. Callahan's clean as far as any police record goes. I checked him out after the first time I bought a book there—just out of curiosity. I think he's just what he says he is—a retired school teacher who likes books and can't live on the measly pension he gets. Still, it wouldn't hurt to get him in here tomorrow to look at the rogues' gallery in that clip. The way he reacts might give something away. In any case, he should be able to identify his regulars. Some low-life might have missed the sign or come in before it was chalked on the sidewalk. We can't be sure that Scarlotti was the artist."

"For all we know," said Pete, "some kid made that chalk mark."

"I'll give Callahan a call after the ball game. Is it safe to set up an afternoon date for you to run the film for him?"

"I'll be patrolling in the cruiser then," said Pete, "but Jack will be here. He could run the projector in his sleep."

"Good. Barney's is usually closed on Mondays. He won't lose any sales by coming in."

CHAPTER 11

▼

Monday morning was one of those days best forgotten. A cold wind had moved in from Canada, displacing the balmy weather of the weekend and meeting head on the moisture-laden air current from the southwest. The result, sleet, turned late May into February except that the sleet melted the moment it hit the ground.

Charlie Witherspoon glanced out of a conference room window in the faculty office building. Libertino had wanted to question the students at headquarters but finally agreed the informal atmosphere at the law school might make the students more willing to talk. Besides, he had been unable to arrange for any official room large enough to hold four people comfortably. All Charlie could see was the drab gray stone of the south wing of Langdell Hall, dismal in the best of weather and now downright depressing. He turned to look at Rosie and Libertino.

Libertino said, "Bell, Brooke, and Chandler—what a great name for a law firm if they should ever decide to practice law together." He was referring to the three third-year students they had been questioning over the past ninety minutes. Chandler, the last of the three, had just left the room. "I must say their stories agree. They didn't sound rehearsed, either."

Charlie sighed, "You don't know the half of it. There's a Chicago law firm of that name—the one I'm a junior partner in. They happen to be sons of the founders. Thank God they seem to be in the clear of both cheating and Fisher's murder. I doubt that I'd have agreed to help with the investigation if I'd known they were involved. The Dean would have had problems too. Bell senior gave five million dollars to the law school last year."

"Their story is not unusual," Rosie said. "Five law students, members of a study group, holed up in a Boston hotel the night before an exam. No one left the hotel Thursday night.

"Friday morning early is a little more uncertain because they all went to bed about four a.m. Someone might have sneaked out to kill Fisher and have managed to get back in the hotel room without being noticed," said Charlie.

"That assumes he knew about Endicott's party and that Fisher would be there," said Rosie.

"From what I've heard," said Libertino, "Everyone within a fifty-mile radius of Cambridge knew about Endicott's party. Fisher's presence there is another matter. In my judgment someone followed him there or met him at the party by accident and seized the opportunity to kill him. Another problem with any of these three students is the time of death. The M.E. is usually right within his stated limits, particularly when he gets a fresh corpse to examine. He gave the limits as three a.m. and five a.m. None of these law students had a car at the hotel. At that time of the morning it would take nearly an hour to get from the Kenmore to Inman Avenue on foot. The MTA doesn't run at that hour. Even if he was lucky enough to find a cab, he'd be crazy to take the risk. Still, it's part of the routine to check out the cab company logs, the night clerk at the Kenmore, and Parsons and Edwards, the other two members of the study group. Unless there's some surprise testimony, we can rule out Bell, Brooke and Chandler. Incidentally, Professor, why aren't we questioning Parsons and Edwards?"

"They both did very well on the essay part of the exam and not so well on the true-false part. Besides, both of them were in the bathroom off and on from five a.m. on—the upper and lower Tasmanian come-aparts. Neither one would have had the strength to get down to the lobby and hail a cab." Rosie turned to Charlie. "How much nepotism is there in that law firm of yours? Bell, Brooke and Chandler are all only C students, C+ at best. Can they count on being hired by the firm and making partner? If they can, why bother to cheat?"

Charlie said, "Remember that merely getting in to this law school and graduating is something of an achievement. The further you go from Cambridge, the more the Harvard name means. They're sure to get jobs and partnerships so long as they keep their noses clean."

There was a knock on the door. Libertino said, "Come in." The student who entered looked as if he had just arrived from County Cork. He was lean and wiry with blue eyes in a face that shouted blarney, topped with flaming red hair.

"Francis Xavier Kirby, at your service," he said, then laughed when he saw Rosie. "Professor, I owe you an apology."

"I was hoping to keep that incident quiet," said Rosie. "I might as well tell it my way." He looked at Libertino. "Exams here are loosely proctored as a rule, sometimes not at all. The professor himself rarely shows up. He gets one of the teaching fellows to pass out the printed questions and blue books and comes back three hours later to pick up the answers."

Kirby said, "But you were there, prof, last Friday, during the entire three hours."

"Yes, I was concerned for two reasons. First, a true-false test was unusual, if not unprecedented. Second, I'd had an anonymous phone call the morning of the exam. The caller said someone was selling the answers, then hung up. The voice sounded muffled. I never could have identified it."

"He probably spoke through a handkerchief," said Witherspoon.

"At any rate," continued Rosie, "I dismissed the call at the time as a prank. The security was tight on the printed questions, and no one but me had a copy of the answers. By starting time, though, I'd become uneasy. No one would dream of cheating on an essay question; it would be too obvious and take too long. On true-false questions, however, a good student in the front of the room could signal the rest of the class by the way he lay his pencil down or how high he raised it. This might happen even if no one had bought the answers."

"You certainly looked suspicious to me," said Kirby.

"To come to the point," said Rosie, wagging his finger at Kirby, "this good-for-nothing Irishman pulled out a large silver pocket watch, opened the cover, and appeared to refer to it frequently as he filled in his blue book."

"Sure, and it was an heirloom me fayther brought from Ireland," said Kirby in an overdone brogue.

"Quiet, young man!" said Rosie. "Let me tell this outrageous story my way. I was taken in hook, line and sinker. I approached him quietly from the back of the lecture room and asked him what time it was. He looked up at the wall clock and said, '3:10.' I said I'd like to check the time by his pocket watch. Kirby got it out and opened the cover to let me read, 'Fooled you again, you old fossil!' It's bad enough to be taken in by a trick like that in front of a room full of law students, but what really hurts is to be called an old fossil before I'm forty."

Charlie Witherspoon let out one gigantic guffaw before he was able to control himself. "Your story reminds me of a stunt pulled by my college roommate, Hans Ritter. Hans came from Milwaukee German stock, in a family that still spoke German every day at meals. His German-born grandmother, who had lived with the family since before Hans was born, never spoke anything else. Hans could manage conversational German very well. Spelling and grammar were his Achilles heel. After the college exam Hans was called in to explain why he had done so poorly—in fact he had turned in a blank bluebook except for the cover page. The prof, in a feeble attempt at humor, had given him ten points 'for neatness and brevity.'"

"How did he get out of that one?" asked Kirby.

"Hans explained that in any exam he always filled out and signed the cover pages of two bluebooks, sure that he would, use both to display his immense knowledge. It was simply insurance against being unable to find another blue-book in a hurry when he needed one. This time he wrote everything he had to say in one bluebook, turning one in and throwing the other in the wastebasket. He told the prof he must have thrown away the wrong one. The prof believed his story—it had never been used before—and gave him his classroom grade, which was based almost entirely on conversation and translation, a respectable B average."

"What colossal brass!" said Kirby, admiringly. His eyes revealed wheels turning within his devious brain.

"Too bad," said Rosie. "You have only one more exam to take before you're a graduate lawyer. Remember, there's no such thing as a classroom average in this law school."

"Where were you last Thursday night?" asked Libertino. His tone said, let's get down to business.

Kirby said, "I don't see that my whereabouts has anything to do with the evidence exam, but I have nothing to hide. I went to the movies—Bogie and Bergman in Casablanca—right here in Harvard Square."

"The movies on the night before an exam?" asked Libertino in disbelief.

"Sergeant, I've tried it the hard way—staying up all night to cram. It just doesn't work for me. I do better if I do a reasonable amount of review once a month during the school year. Then when exam time comes, I just relax and enjoy it."

"Did you see the early or late show?" continued Libertino.

"I was there between nine watch and eleven watch. Aren't you going to ask me to describe the plot?"

"How many times have you seen that movie?" asked Witherspoon suspiciously. He sensed he'd met another Bogart buff.

"Fifteen, including television reruns," replied Kirby. "They usually cut something on television which should be a capital offense. Even so, each time I see it I see at least one nice touch that I'd missed before."

"Okay, okay," said Libertino, looking at his watch in exasperation. "You didn't go to Endicott's party?"

"No."

"You knew about it?"

"Of course. John Rogers, who lives downstairs from Endicott, is a close friend—same class. I had more sense than to go to one of Endicott's blasts the night before an exam. There's such a thing as too much relaxation."

"The movie's not much of an alibi," said Libertino.

"No, it isn't," agreed Kirby, "and my place is only a ten-minute walk from the Inman Avenue apartment. But Sergeant, I had no reason to kill Fisher."

"You knew him?"

"Barely. John Rogers introduced him once, claimed that Fisher had really helped him with his first year courses. It could be true. John was asked to join law review."

"Were you ever tutored by Fisher?" asked Libertino.

"No," said Kirby. "I've always stood on my own two feet. I get mostly C's with a sprinkling of B's—not great, but good enough to put me in the top third of the class."

"Those grades won't get you a job with a top firm," said Charlie, "at least not in the Northeast."

"In a top law firm, they expect you to work seventy hours a week," said Kirby. "Who wants to do that? I've no intention of practicing law. I'm going into the family business. My father insisted on the legal training as background. He claims it takes a thief to catch a thief."

"Why not business school?" asked Rosie.

"My older brother's already been there, a Baker scholar over there on the wrong side of the river."

"How do you explain your top grade on my true-false test?" asked Rosie."

"I had a feeling I'd done well," said Kirby, "and it's nice to have it confirmed. That sort of test has always been duck soup for me. I can literally smell the answer from the wording of the question."

After Kirby left, Libertino said, "I think he was telling the truth. Why should he call all that attention to himself with that crazy watch stunt if he had been planning to cheat?"

"It could be a double bluff," said Charlie.

"You've been reading too many detective stories," said Libertino. "In real life, the simple explanation is the right one nine times out of ten."

"I agree," said Rosie. "Why should he take the risk? Unless a student had come to me with the story that the answers were for sale. I never would have gone over the exam results with a fine-tooth comb. Even then I was inclined to discount the story. I *still* have my doubts."

"You just don't want to believe that your secretary's involved," said Charlie.

"That's part of it," Rosie admitted. "I'm going back to Columbia right after graduation. The Dean tells me there will never be another true-false test at this law school. Why make it difficult for Emily Quince? At the worst she was guilty of an indiscretion or negligence. I can't believe she conspired with Fisher."

"Where is this Quince woman now?" asked Libertino.

"She's up in New Hampshire. Her father's recovering from a stroke and has just been released from the hospital. Emily went up to take over until she could arrange for a housekeeper. The old boy must be made of teak. The doctors think he'll make a complete recovery."

Libertino said, "I want to see that woman the minute she gets back. I suppose here would be less embarrassing than the police station."

"Emily would die at the thought of being seen in the custody of the police," said Rosie. "You're barking up the wrong tree. She was apparently spending some time with Fisher, Perhaps there was a romantic attachment, but she had no motive for killing him."

"It's just one step from love to hate," said Libertino, trying to sound profound. "In any case, Fisher may have told her something important. Are we ready for Mr. Flaherty? Professor, you're nearest the door. See if he's out there."

Rosie opened the door. A subdued Kevin Flaherty sat in one of the captain's chairs in the hallway. In the other sat the buxom brunette Rosie remembered from the party—the one with the tape measure.

Kevin looked up. He seemed strangely embarrassed. "This is Bev Carter. She insisted on coming with me."

"Come in, Kevin," said Rosie. "Miss Carter, would you mind staying where you are for the time being?"

Inside the room with the door closed, Rosie said to Libertino, "Kevin brought a Miss Carter with him. I believe she was his date for the party Tom Endicott gave. I assumed we would want to talk to Kevin alone first."

Libertino scowled. "Let's get her in now, too. Sometimes you can tell more by their facial expressions, watching one while the other is talking. Besides, they've had three days to practice their stories." The truth was he was tired of questioning these wiseacre students. They seemed to be getting nowhere.

Kevin spoke up, "Before you let her in, please ask me any questions you have about the exam. She insisted on coming because she can give me an alibi. That won't be necessary if I can satisfy you some other way."

"You know why you're here?" asked Rosie.

"The Dean's secretary said it was at his invitation. She didn't elaborate. I gathered it was a command performance. Of course, it's common knowledge that cheating is suspected on the evidence exam, and that the cheating is somehow connected with Fisher's death. I guess I'm the only person who took the exam who also lives in the apartment where Fisher died. I suppose that makes me a prime suspect."

"Had you ever met Fisher?" asked Libertino.

"Not until the night of our party," said Kevin. "I didn't really meet him then. I was just aware of his being there and wondered who he was. He wasn't a professor and certainly not a student. He seemed out of place. It did occur to me that he might have walked in off the street without an invitation. Stranger things have happened at our parties."

"You realize that your answers to the true-false part of the exam were identical with a set found in Fisher's apartment?" Rosie continued.

"I didn't know that. It's only a coincidence."

Libertino interrupted. "Let's hear the alibi. If we can rule him out on Fisher's death, I'm going home. The rest of you can go on about the exam as long as you like. I'm sorry to involve your girlfriend, but I don't see any other way."

Kevin said," The night of the party, we locked ourselves in my bedroom about midnight. My roommate is in the infirmary with mumps; there was no one to disturb us. The party was still going full blast. Fisher had apparently passed out. He was lying on the living room floor covered by a bedspread."

"How long were you in the bedroom?"

"Until nearly nine the next morning."

"You must have left the apartment just before I got there," said Libertino accusingly.

"Look, Sergeant, neither of us had anything to do with Fisher's death. Can you blame me for getting the hell out of the place when I knew the police were on their way? I didn't want to advertise the fact that she spent the night here. We weren't exactly playing gin rummy."

Libertino opened the door, and Bev nearly fell into the room. She obviously had been listening with amusement to Kevin's account.

Rosie said, "Kevin, I'm proud of you. It's refreshing in these days of cynicism to find a young man who worries about a lady's reputation."

"I can take care of that myself, Professor," said Bev, not the least bit embarrassed. "That may have been Kevin's motive, but you guys simply don't understand today's woman. To bed a Harvard law student on the first date and inspire him to perform five times in one night is a real achievement. I'm proud of myself and of him. My friends are demanding introductions."

Kevin looked away, blushing. Libertino realized he might have had other reasons for keeping Bev out of the room.

"I move to dismiss all charges," said Charlie. "The defendant would have been too tired to do anything more that night."

"Let's call it a day," said Libertino. "We've done damn little today except to eliminate all the suspects.

On the way out Rosie said to Charlie, "I'm just as glad we didn't turn up anything incriminating. I'd like to believe none of the students cheated and Fisher's murder had nothing to do with the law school."

"Take off those Rosie-colored glasses," said Charlie.

Kevin had borrowed Pete van Pelt's car to take Bev back to Wellesley. He was trying to cover up his embarrassment from the session at the law school. "Do you remember that old saying about the peerage? Once a duke, always a duke; once a knight, that's enough."

CHAPTER 12

▼

Jack Boyle wondered for the umpteenth time why he had ever joined the police force. In a way, he had taken the path of least resistance by following the example of three older brothers. Also he rather fancied himself in the uniform. He expected to be out in the jungle, thwarting dangerous criminals. When they found out he had a sound knowledge of photography and could run projectors of all kinds with the pictures right-side up and in focus, his fate was sealed. On this bleak Monday he was actually enjoying the job of running the videotape with the shots of Barney's Bookstore.

Bill Collins and Callahan, the owner of the store, were seated close to the screen even though Boyle had told Collins many times that any frame could be blown up to show greater detail. He would be able to do even better if he could talk Collins and the chief into buying some equipment that had just come on the market.

"Be sure to freeze the action when I tell you, Jack," said Collins.

"Certainly, Lieutenant." Boyle resented being told how to do his job, especially by a man who knew practically nothing about cameras or projection techniques. Still, talking back to Collins was the best way to wind up walking a beat in the worst part of North Cambridge. Just then Jack Boyle's own homely face appeared on the screen, stooping in front of the doorway to the bookstore.

"Obviously a hardened criminal type," said Collins. "Look at that low, sloping forehead, eyes set too far apart, and those ears sticking out. Seriously, Jack, what made you bend over just then?"

"One shoelace was loose. Also, I was curious about a strange mark in yellow chalk on the sidewalk just in front of the door."

The next subject was the woman with the gray coat and the Paisley scarf. At Collins' command, Boyle ran the tape in slow motion. In the frames before the yellow chalk appeared, her body was blocking a view of the sidewalk in front of the door—it certainly would have been possible for her to have made the mark.

"You've helped with one thing," said Collins. "I was wondering whether she had made that mark. No way, since it was there when you went into the store ahead of her."

"She's a regular,' said Callahan. "Michelle Colbert, an operating room nurse at Mass. General. I don't know anyone more respectable."

"I thought I saw her talking to you in back of the counter," said Boyle.

"That would be true any time she came in. She's a woman who always has something to say."

"Is there any other kind?" asked Collins. "How long have you known her?"

"Three years."

Soon they got into a rhythm as each new face appeared at the entrance to Barney's. Boyle would stop the projector at a frame which would provide a good shot of the subject's face—if the cameraman had been able to get one.

Callahan, who claimed to have a good memory for faces, said he had never seen before more than half of that day's customers. "A lot of the so-called customers only browse. Unless they buy something I may never get to talk to them. You know it first hand, Lieutenant. You're one of my Saturday morning regulars. How many of these people are familiar to you?"

"Only a few, Mr. Callahan," said Collins, "but my interest in people's faces is limited. I'd recognize anyone in the drug business who's on our books. Also, I'd spot a regular user, specially one who was overdue for a fix. There's something in the jerky way they move."

When they finished with the last subject, Boyle turned on the lights.

Collins turned off the flashlight he'd been using to make notes. "Let me see. According to my notes, twenty-seven characters came into the store—you recognized only twelve and could put names to only five of those."

"That sounds right," said Callahan. "Sorry I couldn't be more helpful."

"You did your best. Some witnesses are so obliging, they make things up to please the police. That we can do without. Thank you for coming in, Mr. Callahan."

When Callahan was safely out of earshot, Collins asked, "What did you think of him, Jack?"

"I think he was holding something back. He and that French chick were as thick as thieves, whispering behind the counter. He seemed surprised to see me today. I'll bet he had no idea I was on the force."

"I dunno, Jack. It could be that he has the hots for her. I've seen him turn on the charm for any good looker who comes into his store. The gals go for his technique, too. Take it from me. What about the other customers in the store when you were there. Did any of them seem tense, wild-eyed, excited—in need of a fix?"

"I didn't notice anything like that. Of course, I was minding my own business, going through some paperbacks. I had no idea the place was staked out. It wasn't like I was on duty. Hell, I wasn't in there more than thirty minutes."

"A good police officer is always on duty," said Collins, pompously. "When you read about an arrest in the newspapers, half the time it was made by an officer who was off duty." Collins shook his head. "I don't believe it. If there had been any junkies going in to that store, something would have showed on the video. The subjects didn't know they were on camera—no reason for them to be on their guard at the entrance to the store. Besides, only amateurs would hand the stuff out in a public place like that. Junkies are much more likely to be noticed than. someone up the ladder in the distribution chain—a dealer who's not on the stuff himself."

"You think Barney's is some kind of wholesale distribution point?"

"For a greenhorn, you're not so dumb," said Collins. "Something went wrong last Saturday. The expected shipment didn't come in. For a day or two the shock waves spread over the city—Boston too—because the wholesalers were out and the users didn't get their usual. There were breakins in pharmacies, doctors' offices, any place that might have drugs. One character in a ski mask even went into the Mt. Auburn emergency room waving a forty-five."

"What happened?" asked Boyle.

"A police ambulance had just delivered a knifing victim. The driver and his sidekick waited until the junkie went out the door; then they jumped him. He'd put the gun back in his pocket to pop a few pills. Nobody was hurt. By Monday, the guys who are running this show worked out a substitute channel and things are back to normal. At least the violence is down."

"What do you suppose happened on Saturday?"

"My guess is that a different book or music store is used each week. Either a truck got hijacked or a wrong signal went out. When Scarlotti didn't get any response, he realized there'd been a slipup. He'd warn off the others."

Boyle said, "There's a certain genius in using a book or music store. People hang around without buying anything,"

"Last year there was a beaut of a plan using a Chinese laundry," said Collins. "The pusher went to one place to pay his money and get a ticket. Then he went to the laundry and swapped the ticket for a package of dope wrapped up like a shirt."

Boyle nodded appreciatively. "That way there were no drugs in the store when the cash was paid. Why didn't they just mail out the tickets?"

"Use your head," said Collins. "None of these pushers wanted to give an address, 'specially an address where they really lived. The narcs could have someone working in the post office. For the same reason a post office box would be dangerous, and what if some idiot put the stuff in the wrong box? Besides the buyer wants something to show for his money when he pays over the cash. The little guy would like to go back to the old ways—a direct swap of money for dope. If he can't get that, he wants something to hold onto—no way is he going to wait for the postman."

"How did Scarlotti happen to go to Barney's in the first place?" asked Boyle.

"The Swenson tape is a real help there."

"I thought that tape was a complete garble," said Boyle. "I know that Pete was going to try to clear it up this week. He didn't have the parts he needed to complete a filter he was making."

"He remembered a ham radio friend with a good stock of spares. Pete was up most of the night putting the damn filter together and trying it out. He managed to get a fairly clean audio from the tape."

"Who was Swenson talking to in the bar?" asked Boyle.

"We're pretty sure it was Tony the Scar. The voice certainly sounds like his, and he mentions Barney's by name. We understand the bartender can confirm it was Scarlotti, but we haven't been able to run him down yet. Swenson calls the character he's talking to 'Bill', but that don't prove nothing."

"He wouldn't call him by his real name, would he?"

"Maybe and maybe not," said Collins. "Scarlotti may have been posing as someone else and Swenson may not have known his real name. I do know that Swenson had been posing as a man with access to large quantities of the real stuff—highest quality. From the tape it's clear that Tony was on to something and was trying to cut himself in on the action one way or another. He was trying to pump Swenson just as hard as Swenson was trying to pump him."

"How much did Swenson learn?" asked Boyle.

"Scarlotti found out that some kind of musical password was used in the distribution scheme. We've got the word out to arrest Scarlotti on sight. I'm afraid we're going to be too late."

"What makes you think so?"

"Tony was trying to muscle in, and this crowd is quick on the trigger. Remember what happened to the spade last week, the one they found in a car trunk in Porter Square?"

"Isn't it possible Scarlotti was just one of the regular dealers going in to pick up his supplies for the week?"

"I don't think so from the clumsy way he went about it," said Collins. "I'm convinced that Barney's was supposed to be the drop point, either for dope or some kind of ticket. For some reason the shipment didn't arrive. Maybe Tony didn't have the code quite right, or perhaps he didn't approach the right person. Either way, Callahan is not in the clear yet."

CHAPTER 13

▼

As the senior tenant in the ground-floor Inman Avenue apartment, John Rogers rated the only bedroom with just one bed. Charlie Witherspoon sat on the desk chair, and for want of anything better, Tom Endicott leaned against the window sill. Rogers himself was sitting up in bed wearing a purple silk robe emblazoned with the imperial seal of the Romanoffs. He was inordinately proud of this garment, picked up at a bargain in a church thrift shop. Parts of his face were the same color as the robe.

"This is the first time you've been really awake since we brought you home from the hospital," said Tom.

"I know. I've taken only one Demoral today. Yesterday I had three—I was in real agony. Thanks for the chicken soup by the way. If you ever decide to be a Jewish mommy, I'll be glad to furnish references."

"Tell Charlie what you told me this morning," said Tom.

"About six months ago I met a guy in the Oxford Grille. He called himself Martin Fleming, a name that somehow seemed phony even at the time. He was wearing an old turtleneck sweater, hair almost shoulder length, and horn-rimmed glasses. I had an impression of an older man trying to look like one of the younger faculty."

"How did he move?"

"I saw him only sitting down. He used his hands a lot while he talked. His movements were rapid and jerky, like he was playing a part."

"What did you talk about?" asked Charlie.

"He knew about my part-time radio job as a disc jockey," said Rogers. "He said he wanted to play a joke on some friends. He knew that every Friday night near eleven o'clock I played what I called my mystery selection, usually a piano piece lasting only a few minutes, always something classical. I never announce the piece, the composer, or the artist until the piece is finished."

Rogers continued, pausing to drink a glass of water. "Fleming said that he and some friends regularly had a few drinks at the bar there every Friday night along with Harvard types who thought they were the last word in culture and refinement. Fleming wanted to impress them with his superior knowledge of music. He wanted to rig it just once so that he would know in advance what was going to be played. He wanted to pick the recording himself to make it a stinker to recognize."

Charlie said, "In any bar I've ever been in, some jock has the TV on watching some ball game. You wouldn't have a chance of hearing the radio if there was one."

"The bartender at the Grille is real long hair about music. He lets the jocks watch anything they like in the early evening, but when my program, 'Night Music,' comes on at eleven, he turns off the TV and turns up the radio so that you can hear it anywhere in the place until closing time. Fleming's plan was to give the mystery selection a run of about fifteen seconds then impress his friends by announcing not only the name of the piece and the composer, but the artist as well."

Tom Endicott spoke up. "I have an uncle who is that way about wine. One taste and he'll tell you the type, the year, the estate where the wine was bottled and that the grapes were late grapes grown on the northern slope."

Charlie frowned at this interruption. He was proud of his average at blindfold wine tasting contests in Chicago. "Was Fleming insistent that his piece be played on a Friday night?" he asked Rogers.

"He asked about Thursday. I told him I usually worked only Mondays and Fridays. So we settled on Friday."

"Why did he insist on making the selection himself? Why couldn't you phone him after you'd made the selection from what was available at the station?"

"I think he was afraid I'd play some old chestnut that anyone could recognize. Now that I think of it in context, that argument doesn't hold water. The very first thing he wanted me to play was a movement from a well-known Beethoven sonata—I forget which one. I knew we had a tape of it at the station. It was a Thursday night that we first met at the Grille. He wanted me to play the Beethoven thing the next evening. It was a composition that fit the mood of the program, so I thought, 'What the hell. It's an easy way to make 25 bucks, and it's only a one-shot proposition.'"

"It became a regular thing, though. Didn't it?" asked Charlie.

Rogers smiled sheepishly, "It was such an easy thing to do for the money compared what I had to do to scrounge a few bucks elsewhere. Fleming would call me on Thursday afternoon to give me the selection. I'd use it Friday night as my mystery piece, and Saturday morning without fail twenty dollars in cash would be in an, envelope in our mailbox. There never was a stamp on the envelope. It must be hand-delivered. I've had a few moral twinges. I suppose that he's ripping off his friends by betting on a sure thing. Maybe I'm rationalizing, but I figure those Harvard types can afford it."

Charlie asked, "How could he be sure that the station had the record or tape that he selected?"

"I xeroxed our lists and gave him copies."

"What happened last Friday night?" asked Charlie. "I remember hearing part of your mystery selection myself, just as I was leaving Chancery Club."

"I had problems," said Rogers. "Fleming had picked a Chopin mazurka which happened to be on a record rather than on a tape. The tape cassettes are practically foolproof—shove them in a slot and push a button. A lot of things can go wrong with a record or turntable. As I got the record out of its jacket just before air time, I knocked over my mug and spilled coffee on one side of the record. I had to improvise. On the flip side was another Chopin mazurka, played by the same pianist, Orazio Frugoni. That's what I played. There was no way to get word to Fleming in time. I figured if he missed the number of the mazurka by only one it would lend credibility to his performance. The coffee made the other side of the record at least temporarily unplayable. There wasn't time to clean it up properly and test it. If I hadn't had cream in my coffee I might have tried it."

"You were beaten up because you played one Chopin mazurka rather than another?" asked Charlie incredulously. "Exactly what did those thugs say to you?"

"Neither of them said anything until just as they left. Then the big guy—the one who's good at kicking you when you're down—said, 'That's just a taste of what you'll get if you don't play the right number next time.' I didn't connect what he said with the radio program at first. The mention of playing the number made me think of the gambling rackets. I thought they had mixed me up with somebody else, some other poor sucker who owed money to a loan shark, perhaps."

"Probably that's who their usual victim was," said Tom.

"How did you ever meet a character like Fleming?" asked Charlie.

"Lawrence Fisher introduced us," said Rogers.

"Why didn't you say so in the first place?"

"I didn't think it was important," said Rogers. "Fisher was never around when Fleming and I talked about the radio program. Even the first time when the three of us met in the Oxford Grille Fleming made some excuse to get rid of Fisher. Fisher was curious, obviously reluctant to go but afraid to defy Fleming. Fleming is not the sort of person who shares confidences. I think he was afraid Fisher might spoil his practical joke."

"Practical joke! My friend, if all Fleming was up to was a practical joke, why did he hire those goons to rough you up? The same question applies if he was winning a few bucks from friends. Some bigger game's afoot, as Sherlock used to say. I'm sorry. There's no way we can keep this information from the police, and I know Libertino will want to hear it first hand."

"Try to keep me out of it," said Tom. "I think the sergeant is just looking for an excuse to throw me in a cell."

CHAPTER 14

▼

Libertino was in a good mood even though the weather was still lousy. He and Gina finally managed to get on more or less the same schedule, so they could spend more time in bed together. He wondered how he ever managed before he met her. The dividend was that she responded to his enthusiastic love-making not only in bed but also by turning out culinary triumphs drawn from an amazing repertoire taught her by a Milanese mother and a Roman grandmother.

The sergeant was delighted to get something new to work on in the Fisher case. Even though the murder was only a week old, it had the smell of staleness about it. In the easy cases, mused Libertino, something broke in the first two or three days. The husband or lover confessed. The beady-eyed woman across the street called in to report something crucial, and the case practically solved itself. Here there had been no breaks, and from past experience Libertino knew the odds were the case would quickly go into the inactive file. Now, with the link to Fleming, there was a chance.

Libertino was back at his desk in Central Square after questioning John Rogers at his apartment and stopping at the radio station to get a list of the mystery selections over the past six months. A very obliging young lady at the station had been able to dig this information out of their files and assemble it with Witherspoon's help. Charlie had been invited along as the classical music expert. The sergeant was abysmally ignorant in this area and Tom Endicott not much better. Besides, Tom was champing at the bit to meet Tina.

Libertino and Witherspoon were looking at copies of the list of musical selections. Charlie said, "They seem mostly to be fairly short piano pieces, heavy on

Chopin with a sprinkling of Bach, Beethoven,and Liszt. It's odd there's absolutely nothing by Mozart."

"I don't get it," said Libertino. "The number Rogers was supposed to play was Chopin's Mazurka No. 13. He plays number five instead, and somebody beats the living shit out of him?"

"Same composer, same type of piece, same pianist," said Witherspoon, "just different keys and different opera."

"What do you mean, 'opera'?" asked Libertino. "There's nobody singing, is there?"

"The plural of opus is opera," said Charlie. "I'll be damned if I'll say opuses."

"In any case," said Libertino, "the difference between the two pieces got Rogers beaten up and may somehow be connected with Fisher's death. It's too bad we haven't got more on Fleming—not even a first name, and a description that's practically worthless when you discount the long hair and glasses which are probably part of a disguise. There are fifteen Flemings in the phone book, one spelled with a final 'S'." We'll check them out as a matter of routine. I have a gut feeling it'll be a wild goose chase."

"Was there anything in Fisher's papers to suggest any musical angle?" asked Witherspoon.

"I don't remember a damned thing, but I must say I had no reason to look for one. I've sent for Fisher's papers and personal effects. They've been in a carton in the basement."

"Did Fisher have any heirs?" asked Charlie,

"No one's come forward, and we've found no trace of a will. Fisher apparently lived pretty well up to his income. The estate may be barely enough to satisfy his creditors."

Detective Hennessey came through the doorway and put a carton on the desk. Beside it be laid a slim, black book with an imitation leather cover. "I did what you told me to, Joe. I went through the clothes again and found this."

"Something you didn't find the first time?" said Libertino, glaring at both Hennessey and the black notebook.

"Have a heart, Sarge," said Hennessey. "It slipped down through a tear in the lining of the jacket. I wouldn't have found it this time if the jacket hadn't fallen out of the carton. I felt something stiff in there when I picked it up."

"Let's see what you've got there," said Libertino. "It looks like the little black book my buddy used to carry in the army. He seemed to be able to get a date in any city in the country. Damn it! It's just a pocket calendar. Wait a minute, he kept his appointments in it."

"Let's check the Fridays when Rogers was broadcasting," said Charlie.

"That's strange. There are some kind of musical symbols followed by a name."

Charlie went around to look at the notebook over Libertino's shoulder. He became excited. "Musical keys!" he said. "The keys of the mystery selections. Look at the box for the first Friday in February: B flat Barney's; the next Friday, C is Conway's; then F sharp, Fletcher's."

"They're all names of bookstores," said Hennessey.

"I didn't know you could read," said Libertino. "Barney's I recognize. It's been around a long time. Where are the others?"

"Conway's is in Central Square on a side street you could easily miss. Fletcher's is near North Station," said Hennessey.

Charlie Witherspoon's face lit up like a thousand watt bulb just turned on inside his head. "Are you guys willing to accept help from a woman?"

"I'd take help from the devil himself," said Libertino.

"Dorothy Sayers, a scholarly English woman who wrote in the twenties and thirties, created Lord Peter Wimsey, the younger brother of a duke who solved crimes as a hobby. In *Murder Must Advertise*, my favorite, a drug distribution system is run from a London. advertising agency. The syndicate has a man inside the agency who tips them off each week, tells them in advance the headline in a newspaper ad. If the headline is 'Nutrax for Nerves,' for example, the first letter of the headline is the key to where the dealer can pick up his weekly allotment. He has a telephone book with certain pubs ticked off. He looks for the first one beginning with an 'N' and shows up there with a copy of the newspaper folded to show the Nutrax ad. If necessary, he makes a remark about the product. Somebody shoves a package into his jacket or coat pocket."

"Sounds complicated to me," said Libertino. "Still, I've heard of stranger arrangements. Hennessey, go across the hall and see if Collins can spare us a few minutes. Tell him we may have a lead on how the horse is being dealt here."

Later Collins began to get excited, too. "Let me see if I understand what Fisher figured out—what probably got him killed. If the key of the mystery selection was B, they'd be dealing dope that Saturday at the first bookstore under B in the Yellow Pages. The number Rogers was supposed to play last Friday was a Mazurka in the key of A. He plays one in B instead, so Tony the Scar shows up at Barney's instead of Armstrong's. He or someone else warns off the dealers when the gang finds out about Rogers' goof."

"It may not be that simple," said Charlie. "The dealers may be using marked phone books so that the choice of bookstores is much narrower. Also, the musical key may not be the critical clue. It could be the opus number or the number of the mazurka, ballade or whatnot."

"Look, Witherspoon," said Collins. "I was in Barney's last Saturday. I know something fishy was going on. My nose tells me we're on the right track. When will Rogers know the mystery number for this week?"

"Not until late Thursday afternoon, possibly Friday morning, when he'll get a phone call from Fleming," said Charlie.

"We'll tap the line," said Collins, "try to trace it. Fleming will probably use a pay phone which will make it tougher to trace. At least we can stake out the right bookstore."

$$* \qquad * \qquad * \qquad *$$

Later, Charlie telephoned John Conover, the senior partner in his Chicago law firm.

"Is everything under control, John?"

"We're managing surprisingly well without you. I've been keeping an eye on the Wharton case for you. There's no chance of its coming to trial this month. The judge is in the hospital for a gall bladder operation." The Wharton case had been delayed by pretrial proceedings for more than two years. Two different associates had worked with Charlie on the case—but at different times—and there was no partner with Charlie's close knowledge of the case.

"What's happened in the murder case you called about earlier?" continued Conover. "The one that may be connected with cheating on an exam? I'm sure such a thing would never happen in New Haven. A true-false test, and in a third-year course!" Conover's Yale Law School antecedents always seemed to find a way to surface.

"It was a near thing. Three sons of the founding partners in our firm were under suspicion for a while. Fortunately, they could prove they were in a hotel room during the critical hours, studying for an exam. It's by no means certain now that any cheating took place. The victim, a disbarred lawyer who successfully tutored a number of law students, somehow got hold of the questions on part of an exam and made at least one attempt to sell the answers. However, there's no reliable evidence that a sale ever took place. Also, the police now believe the killing was completely unconnected with any law school exam. The victim was killed to prevent his horning in on a drug distribution scheme or bringing it to the attention of the police. It's a clever system they'd be unlikely to figure out by themselves. I'd like to stay around for a week or two to see how things come out, partly because a close friend of my nephew is involved. Strangely enough, my knowledge of music is proving very helpful to the police."

"Suit yourself, Charlie. You haven't taken a real vacation in two years. You've more than pulled your weight since Cabot and Potter died. I may lean on you a bit in July and August when we're usually shorthanded."

"No sweat," said Charlie. "I like Chicago in July and August so long as I can get in some sailing on the weekends. I'd rather have the time off now."

"Watch out for yourself," said Conover. "You seem to have a talent for attracting danger. Remember the last time you were involved in a murder case—you nearly got yourself killed."

C H A P T E R   15

▼

John Rogers was well enough to get up and sit in a chair part of the next day. The first thing he did was to sharpen all his pencils. He claimed that a well-sharpened pencil was the sign of a keen intellect.

By afternoon he felt even better—well enough to receive a police artist who planned to sketch a portrait from Rogers' description. The problem was that Rogers was only sure about the hair, the glasses, and a moustache, all items that could be part of a disguise. When the artist reported to Collins, the lieutenant shook his head in exasperation. "Average height, average build, didn't notice the color of the eyes—Keerist! It could be anybody." Collins made a mental note to have Rogers look at their rogues' gallery as soon as possible.

*   *   *   *

Back at the hotel, Charlie Witherspoon was bothered by something trying to creep out of his subconscious. He reached for the phone book on the bottom shelf of his bedside table. He turned to the 'Bookstores, Retail' section of the Yellow Pages. There were over two pages of listings, considerably more than 100 entries. If Fisher and Collins were right, the musical key of the mystery selection determined which letter to look under in the bookstore listings. Still, there were only seven letters for the musical keys—unless some maniac had invented a complicated code involving sharps, flats and whether the key was major or minor. In view of the intelligence (or lack of it) of the typical drug dealer, the possibility of misinterpretation was too great. Seven letters might be enough in theory, but Charlie thought it was too limiting.

Another thought occurred to him. An underworld character would stick out like a sore thumb in a posh bookstore that handled only new books, while he would pass unnoticed in the usual secondhand bookstore. The first entries under the musical key letters (A through G) included several stores in the high rent district, stores that wouldn't dream of carrying secondhand books.

Charlie was an amateur musician; he had never even taken a course in music appreciation. His knowledge came mainly from an extensive collection of tapes and records, mostly of classical music and concentrated in the area of piano and chamber music. Chopin was a favorite. His collection included sixty mazurkas, twenty-four preludes, and twenty nocturnes. How often had Chopin been the mystery composer? He reached for his copy of the radio station list. Chopin was well represented, but only three mazurkas had been played over the last six months. They were all in single digit numbers.

The next stop was Widener Library. The college authorities were a bit stuffy about the use of the library by alumni, particularly law school alumni, but so long as you didn't try to take a book out, it was almost impossible to police the use of the reference room. There are stories of people who walked in off the street to get a good education at Widener.

Charlie went to the card catalog. Under music he found several encyclopedias which probably would have served his purpose. As luck would have it, a footnote on each file card explained that the volumes in question were not in the main library but in the branch library at the Music Department. At the desk a user-friendly type looked at Charlie dubiously. Despite his youthful appearance, he couldn't pass for a student and he couldn't produce a card to prove he had paid the 200 dollar user fee for an alumnus. She decided to take pity on him because his face was somehow familiar, and anyway the news was bad.

"I'm sorry," she said. "The Music Department library has just shut down for three weeks."

"How did they know I was coming?" asked Charlie.

Charlie took the Red Line to Park Street and changed for Copley Square. What was the good of having one of the best libraries in the world, perhaps the best, if the books weren't accessible? The Boston Public Library was open, thank God! In the main reference room he found a six-volume musical encyclopedia, just the thing to list the works of the major composers.

No wonder Mozart had not made the list of mystery selections. Unlike the works of most composers, listed by opus number, Mozart's works had been catalogued by Koechel, a German with a teutonic passion for chronology. Mozart was a prolific composer. The shorter pieces, suitable as mystery selections, came in a variety of keys, but the Koechel numbers were all over 200, beyond the available listings of bookstores. What about the opus numbers? Charlie checked the listings for Chopin—a good selection among the suitable short piano pieces, opus—numbers ranging from nine to seventy. One other possibility occurred to him. The code key might be the number of the type of composition, as the "1" in "Sonata No. 1." He went to the record section of the library to look randomly at Chopin labels. Some of them did not even give the key, much less the number of the nocturne, ballade or whatnot—only the opus number, followed by another number if the opus included more than one selection.

He found a pay phone to dial John Rogers at his apartment.

"When you gave the answer to the mystery selection on your disc jockey program, how detailed were you?"

"Fleming was very particular about that. I had to give the composer, number of the type of composition, the key and the opus number. For example, I'd say, 'Chopin's Ballade No. 3 in A Flat Major, Opus 47.' On my own, I always added the name of the recording company and the artist to make it easier for the listener to buy the record or tape."

"What if you didn't find all that information on the label? I've just been looking at labels here at the Boston Public Library, and many of them don't give the dope that Fleming wants."

"Look at the sleeve, man. There's more room there. Then look in the catalogue if you have to."

Charlie thanked him and hung up. He hadn't disproved the Fisher theory, but the Witherspoon theory was looking better all the time. Back to the Yellow Pages. If Rogers' change of selection was reasonable for the goings on at Barney's Bookstore last Saturday, then Barney's should be the seventh bookstore listed to match the opus number of the mazurka. Hell and damnation, Barney's was eighth on the list! He sensed somehow that despite the discrepancy, he was on the right track. Still, it was going to be an uphill battle to convince Collins, a stubborn Irishman if he'd ever met one. He could accept the fact there had been something fishy going on at Barney's, but the disturbance there could have been merely Scarlotti making the same mistake that Fisher and Collins had made— going by the musical key of the composition.

*   *   *   *

Thursday afternoon Collins listened to Charlie in amused patience. Libertino had a knowing look on his face that said, "Collins is digging his heels in; you'll never change his mind."

Collins said, "You amateurs are all alike. Experience is what counts in this business. I was at Barney's last Saturday, and I know there was something criminal going on."

Charlie said, "I'll grant you that Scarlotti was up to no good, but isn't it possible he was in the wrong place because he misread the code?"

"If you're right," said Collins, "why would anyone bother to chalk that yellow symbol on the sidewalk?

"Incidentally," Collins continued, "They found Scarlotti yesterday. He turned up in the Charles in cement overshoes. He's still be at the bottom of the river if some old lady hadn't lost control of her car. She drove right over the embankment into the river. She was damn lucky that a passing jogger was able to get her out of the car in time. Later the diver found Scarlotti when he went in to attach a tow line to the car."

The phone at Collins' elbow rang; he picked it up. "Fleming called Rogers ten minutes ago. Rogers kept him on the line by asking questions—long enough for us to trace the call. It was a pay phone in a Mass Avenue drug store. We got a car over there right away. No one even remotely resembling Fleming was seen in the neighborhood. In fact, the pimply-faced punk behind the drugstore counter didn't remember anyone using the phone. No wonder the crime rate is what it is. At least we know this week's mystery selection—Brahms' Sonata No. 1 in F minor, Opus 120." He reached into the bookcase behind his desk for the Yellow Pages and let his fingers begin their work.

Charlie subconsciously noticed something odd about the cover of the phone book. Before he realized what it was, his attention was distracted by Collins' announcement.

"The first bookstore under F is Fletcher's. I was going to have someone there this Saturday anyhow because of the entry in Fisher's appointment book. Now it rates a full scale stake out."

Charlie picked up the abandoned phone book and counted up to 120 carefully. "My money's on Roxanne's Bookswap," he announced. "The Huntington Avenue address is seedy enough so that anyone can walk in without a coat and tie and feel comfortable. They sell new paperbacks, records, tapes and used books of every description. I'd be tempted to go over to browse tomorrow even if there were nothing criminal going on."

"I'm concentrating on Fletcher's," said Collins. "The full stakeout will include two men inside and three outside with walkie-talkie units ready to follow anyone suspicious. It's a combined operation with Boston because of the Government Center location. We're going to have two squad cars with four more men as back-up. I can't spare anyone just because you have a hunch, but I'll give you a phone number in Boston to call in case of emergency. Huntington Avenue is completely out of my territory, so for Christ's sake don't do nothing stupid. I can see you trying to make a citizen's arrest because you read about it in law school, or worse yet following some pusher down a dark alley. Leave the hero stuff to the guys who are paid to take the risk."

"I wasn't born yesterday," said Charlie with injured dignity.

CHAPTER 16

▼

Charlie stood by the open window of his room at the Commander Hotel. Although the newer part of the hotel had central air conditioning, Charlie had insisted on one of the older rooms with a window unit and a window that would open. There was not a cloud in the sky. It was already hot and humid, unusual for early June. Charlie was glad he had been able to borrow a cotton T-shirt and blue jeans from his nephew, and proud that the jeans were not too tight. He thought they would be less conspicuous if they dressed informally for the trip to the bookstore.

Tom Endicott was waiting for him at a snack bar just off Harvard Square. Charlie would have felt out of place in the Commander's dining room without a coat and tie.

Tom said, "I listened to John's disc jockey program last night. He sounded perfectly natural, not scared to death the way he really was, as he told me later. He took a cab back to the apartment just to be on the safe side. Even then, some seedy character was watching him from across the street as he went into the building. Of course, it may have been just his imagination, but if I'd been beaten up the way he was, my imagination would be pretty lively too."

"It's the old story about closing the barn door after the horse is gone," said Charlie. "Libertino told me they'd have a man watching him, discreetly, or so he said. Naturally I listened to the radio program, too. Fletcher's will be swarming tomorrow with local plainclothesmen and federal agents. Even if it's the right bookstore—which I doubt—any self-respecting criminal will sniff the air and give the place a wide berth."

Charlie heard the counterman repeating an order; it sounded like "sidead-own".

Tom explained. "That means, 'Toast one English muffin.' Don't ask me to explain why."

The counterman spoke again, "Adam and Eve on a raft—wreck 'em."

"That one I get," said Charlie. "Scrambled eggs on toast. Right out of O' Henry if I remember correctly. I'll have to remember this place—juice, eggs, toast and coffee for only $1.50. That's a bargain I haven't seen since my student days. I wish there were something like it in Chicago. What's the best way to get to Rox-anne's? I don't want to take a cab. It would be out of character when we're dressed like this."

Tom laughed, "You look more like a college sophomore than some of the current crop in the Yard. Let's take the Red Line."

"In my day, we called it the subway," said Charlie.

"Not accurate. It's elevated as it crosses the Charles and again as it gets near Quincy."

"Stop nitpicking or someone will call us a 'Quibble of lawyers.' What's the alternative, a bus?"

"We could take a trolley or bus along Mass. Ave. It's shorter in distance, but it would take forever with all the stops, and we might not survive the heat. I don't know why it is. Sometimes the heating system in the MTA cars works only in the summer. Then they can't figure out how to turn it off."

A short time later, they stood in front of Roxanne's Bookstore on Huntington Avenue. They were within a stone's throw of both Northeastern and Harvard Medical School. Tom looked southwest toward the medical school.

"I see we're near one of your old stamping grounds. I've always wondered why you never became a doctor," said Charlie.

"I discovered I simply couldn't stand the sight of blood. Every doctor has to intern at a hospital for a year no matter what specialty he's aiming for. There's no way for the intern to escape duty in the emergency room. A friend told me about a man who came in one night with an ice pick driven through his neck. The intern called for help. Even the old hands didn't know what to do. They took some x-rays, and it looked as if the pick hadn't penetrated any vital spots. Finally, they just pulled the damn thing out, applied some iodine and a Band-Aid, and sent the patient home on his own two feet. All I could think of was that if I'd been there and pulled the ice pick out, buckets of blood would have gushed from the jugular. I resigned at the end of the term."

It was only five after nine—the store had just opened. Charlie said, "Let's go inside. There's really no excuse for hanging around out here. Too bad there isn't a coffee shop across the street where we could sip a second cup of coffee and watch the customers as they go in and come out."

Inside the door a woman in her middle sixties sat behind a long counter, knitting. Her gray hair stuck out from her head in pink, plastic rollers. Her face was thin with a beak instead of a nose. Her clothes were clean but out of style and with obvious mends, probably bought at a church thrift shop. She reminded Charlie of Madame Defarge. He half expected to see the Guillotine in the background.

"Come in, come in," the woman said. "I'm Roxy. You're my first customers this lovely morning. Let me see your hands." Without even thinking of the possibility of refusing this strange request, Charlie and Tom held out their hands for inspection, palms up, and then turned them over in response to her gestures.

"Good," she said. "You both pass. You have no idea how many people come in here with absolutely filthy hands expecting to paw through my nice clean books." She turned to point as she said, "Behind me we have cassettes, a few records, and classical music in book form. The Conservatory is just over there." She indicated a direction with a talon that the Wicked Witch of the West would have been proud of. "Downstairs the fiction starts on the left, alphabetically by author; paperbacks are in the far corner. Non-fiction is on the right, arranged by subject." Her voice and manner suggested someone used to exercising authority.

"Five will get you ten she taught school some place," said Charlie as they went down the stairs.

"No bet," said Tom. "One just like her taught me math in seventh grade. She used to talk about 'West Point discipline.' We were all terrified of her, even the school bully."

The downstairs of Roxanne's was surprisingly cool despite the lack of air conditioning. The English basement front was triple-glazed and shielded by a large canvas awning. Overhead fans with wooden blades moved a large volume of air without sounding noisy. Charlie found a twelve-volume set of *The Golden Bough*, something he had long coveted. "Remember why you're here," said Tom. "How can you follow anyone unobtrusively if you're lugging twelve of those?"

"You could carry six," said Charlie. He hadn't told Tom he was under strict orders from the police not to do any following. "What I could do is take them up to the Holy Terror at the desk, pay for them, and ask her to hold them."

"Okay," said Tom, knowing that his uncle was about to get stubborn. "Van Pelt will be back with his car some time this weekend. We'll get him to pick up your books. It could be better that way. Depending on how things turn out here we may not be popular after today."

Charlie and Tom between them managed to get the heavy set of books up to the desk where Roxy had just finished another row of knitting. She was more than happy to take a twenty-dollar bill from Charlie and give him a receipt. That set of the *Golden Bough* had been on her shelves for years. She thought she was never going to get rid of it.

Out of the corner of his eye Charlie saw a swarthy character leaving the store. Roxy said, "I'll just put these in bundles with red cards to show that they've been sold. We're open until nine tonight, but don't worry if you can't make it. I'll keep them safe for you. I'm here Sunday afternoons from two to four and nine to five Monday through Friday."

When they were far enough down the stairs to be out of Roxy's hearing, Charlie asked, "Did you see that guy in the black hat going out of the store just as Roxy was taking my money? He certainly looks the part of someone on the most-wanted list."

"He may have come in just to pick up a cassette of a Verdi opera," said Tom. "I'm surprised at your bigotry. Just because a man appears to be a refugee from *La Scala* doesn't mean that he's a criminal."

"All the same," said Charlie, "my nose tells me that something is going on upstairs. We'd better split up. You keep watch down here. I'll go back up and browse through the classical music. I can talk a good game if she gets curious. If I spot someone worth following out of the store, I'll flick the light switch at the top of the stairs off and then back on again. Then you get upstairs in a hurry. I'll give you a number to call Collins in case I don't have time to."

"I suppose somebody has to stay out of the action," said Tom. "At least there's a promising collection of detective stories near the stairwell to keep me busy while I'm waiting."

CHAPTER 17

▼

Fletcher's Bookstore was on Cambridge Street more or less opposite the Kennedy Center. With the restoration of the Scollay Square area and Fanueil Market real estate prices had soared, and the decor of the store was in keeping with the exorbitant rent. No expense had been spared in the appointments. The floor was carpeted with an extra-thick pile, providing an excellent sound deadener. Warm fluorescent lights were recessed near the ceiling to bathe the bookshelves in a rosy glow. There were a few trade paperbacks retailing for fifteen dollars or more, but most of the stock was hardcover. Collins thought no one would have enough brass to ask for a discount. At the north end an entire section was devoted to high fidelity equipment with stereo systems starting at one thousand dollars. A prissy young man with carefully styled hair and a flower in his buttonhole presided over an extensive collection of classical tapes and records.

"I'll bet he sits down to take a leak," thought Collins, irreverently. Two plainclothesmen were snarking around trying to be unobtrusive but looking very much like bulls in a stereo shop.

The young man pursed his lips and looked at his watch in annoyance. He looked up and down the aisles of the store, finally spotting a spectacular brunette hurrying toward him.

"Sorry I'm late, Percy," she said.

"I was right," thought Collins. "No real man would have a name like Percy."

Percy said petulantly, "Janet, you knew I had a terribly important luncheon date at Loch Obers. My entire future may depend upon it."

"Come on, Percy, I'm only a few minutes late. If you'd get going instead of standing there complaining, you'd make it with time to spare. Go on, now. If you're really worried, take a cab and I'll pay for it."

"What with Washington Street one-way the wrong way and the time it would take to find a cab, I'll be better off walking," said Percy. He hurried off.

"Now that's a real tomato," thought Collins, "All the curves where they should be and a peaches and cream complexion, probably English." Collins hated the English but admired their women. Surprisingly, her jet-black hair was pulled sharply back from her face into a bun in back of her head. She might have looked school-marmish but for the full, red sensuous lips that promised a thousand and one nights of delight. Collins was enjoying his fantasy until it was interrupted by the approach of a suspicious character.

A tall, distinguished man in clerical garb stood at the counter gazing intently at Janet. Above a Roman collar his face had classic Greek lines topped by a mass of unruly, almost boyish hair with only a touch of gray at the temples.

"Late forties, or maybe early fifties," thought Collins. The clergyman took an envelope from his pocket and handed it to Janet.

"Do you have this Brahms piano sonata on tape, the one with Claudio Arrau?" Collins ears pricked up. "Arrau" was the name that John Rogers had announced as the piano player.

Janet looked at the clergyman and blushed. Then she wrote something on the envelope and handed it back to him. "Let me check our stock, Father," she said and turned to look in some drawers behind the counter.

Collins signaled to one of his men who made heavy-footed haste to join him near the counter. He said, "Keep an eye on that dame, which shouldn't be difficult for a ladies man like you. Don't let her leave the store no matter what her excuse is."

Collins went up to the clergyman and took the envelope in one quick motion from his unresisting fingers.

"I'm Lt. Collins, a police officer. Would you mind stepping back to that empty office in the rear of the store for a quiet discussion?"

"I'm Pierpont Wiggins, a curate at St. John's Episcopal Church." He named an exclusive Boston suburb. He was still in a daze, following Collins without question.

"This makes it easier," thought Collins. Like many lapsed Catholics he still stood in awe of priests and would have found it difficult to question one, much less arrest one. Collins closed the door to the small private office, sat down in the chair behind the desk and motioned to Wiggins to take the only other chair in the room. Then he looked at the writing on the envelope.

"Will you meet me in the choir loft at ten tonight?"

"Yes."

"Can you explain this?" asked Collins. A choir loft seemed an unlikely place to pass out drugs.

Wiggins looked at him shame-facedly. "This is a role reversal for me. In my last parish in Chicago—and I hasten to add that Chicago is the highest diocese in the country—I used to hear confessions every Saturday night. Now I'm about to make one."

"Confessions in the Protestant church?" asked Collins, distracted by this unexpected turn of events.

"Not only confessions, Lieutenant. The clergy were called priests and they had to take vows of celibacy. That was my problem. I've always been oversexed. The Church was definitely the wrong career for a man with my problem. If I had been permitted to marry and found the right sort of wife, I might have made a go of it, although I doubt it. Every time I see a pretty face or halfway decent feminine figure, I lose control. I was dean of the cathedral in another Midwestern city when I got in trouble the first time. It was a choirgirl then, too. Somehow I earned the nickname 'Pinchbottom Wiggins.' Finally, one of the girls complained. That was unusual because I was very much in demand. The bishop gave me another chance by sending me to Chicago as rector of a small suburban church. Within six months I was in trouble again. I would have been unfrocked if the bishop and my mother had not been first cousins. He somehow managed to get me transferred out of his diocese to the Boston area. Now I've been demoted to curate—back where I started out twenty-five years ago."

"I take it you've fallen off the wagon again," said Collins.

"Yes, after six weeks of complete abstinence. It was more than any red-blooded man could stand. I can't control my urges, and the women can't seem to stay away from me."

"Do you have any identification, Father—I mean Mr. Wiggins?"

Wiggins pulled out a driver's license and handed it to Collins, saying, "The address there is the same as the rector's if you want to check it out. I have a small third-floor apartment."

Collins began to wonder whether his choice of bookstores had been correct. He'd been at Fletcher's for more than three hours, and the only suspicious incident turned out to have a more or less innocent explanation.

"How did you come to pick out that particular Brahms sonata?" he asked.

"I happened to hear part of it on the radio last night," said Wiggins. "It was primarily an excuse to talk to the girl and give her my note, but I wouldn't mind having the tape."

"Let's get out of here before the manager returns and demands an explanation," said Collins. "I doubt if I'll have to bother you further."

*   *   *   *

Outside of the bookstore the sound of a church clock striking noon could be heard. Across the street from Fletcher's the plaza area between the Kennedy Center and the New City Hall was already beginning to fill with secretaries and under-paid executives of the brown bag persuasion, along with well-paid overweight executives on a diet. Today was warm enough for the benches in the shade to be taken first.

Two more of Collins men were in the plaza trying not too successfully to blend into the background. One of them had a pushcart full of fruit with his walkie-talkie hidden under a pile of apples. The other was perspiring in a wool hat, a moth-eaten sweater, and faded blue jeans. He was standing nonchalantly near a shoeshine kit, but looked as if he wouldn't know what to do if someone asked for a shine.

A uniformed cop—one of Boston's finest—approached the man with the pushcart. "May I see your peddler's license?" he said.

The detective groaned and shrugged his shoulders in a "you can't win" gesture. He pulled out his identification as a Cambridge police officer.

"We're working the same side of the street," he said, showing his I.D. to the Boston cop.

"Nobody told me you'd be in my territory," said the cop. "I've got a good mind to run you in." He helped himself to an apple.

"Have a heart," said the detective. "Check with your Lt. Kelly in Narcotics. We've got a combined op going with the feds."

Less than fifty feet away a tough ten-year old kid was kicking the shit out of the other detective. "Trying to take over my business, huh?" he said, redoubling his kicks.

"Ouch!" said the detective. "That hurts. Look, you don't understand. It's only for a few hours more. Ouch! What will you take to go away? Ten dollars?"

"Make it a double sawbuck, mister."

The detective winced again as the attack on his shins continued. Collins would never believe him. The twenty bucks would come out of his own pocket.

As a matter of fact he'd left his walkie-talkie on with the transmit switch in "lock" position. Collins, in stunned disbelief, had heard every word.

*   *   *   *

At the edge of the plaza, Fleming, who had just stepped out of Fletcher's, observed the two incidents with ill-concealed amusement. His presence in the store had been completely innocent, as Fletcher's had never been intended as a distribution point for anything. Fleming just happened to be in the neighborhood. When he spotted the stakeout, he stayed around to watch the fun and couldn't resist going in the store. So, they had at least two more men outside, and there were probably some less obvious narcs hanging around in the background. Fleming wore no glasses or wig, only a beret with a jaunty tilt, a charcoal gray flannel suit with a pale blue shirt, and a solid red linen tie. There was little in his appearance except his average height and build to bring to mind the man John Rogers had met at the Oxford Grille. Fleming stopped smiling. While the police were at the wrong place today and behaving ineptly, some day they might stumble on the right bookstore at the right time. Sooner or later they would need a new distribution scheme. If only that bastard Fisher hadn't interfered!

*   *   *   *

Meanwhile back at Roxanne's Bookswap, Charlie Witherspoon was really enjoying himself. He was one of those fortunates who can read musical notes—even those of a complex chord—and hear the separate sounds. This talent had amazed his roommate at Harvard who was a music major but had trouble singing on key. Roxy's collection of piano and organ music was diverse and surprisingly good. He found himself lost in a Bach fugue. The noise of cow bells jangling at the door as a customer entered brought him back to reality.

A nurse in her white working uniform came in carrying an armload of paperbacks.

She looked too attractive to be a real life nurse—more like someone out of "General Hospital".

"She's probably just come off duty," thought Charlie. There were three or four hospitals in the immediate neighborhood.

"Cash or swap?" asked Roxy after giving the books the once-over. "They're in good condition, and you bought them here—that's worth something. I'll give you three dollars in cash or four-fifty in a swap."

"Half cash and half swap," said the nurse in a husky contralto that stirred something in Charlie's inner depths. Roxy handed her an envelope, screening the motion from Charlie with her body. "Here's your cash and your swap coupons; the coupons are good for six months."

Charlie started to move out of his corner to talk to the nurse, but she headed quickly for the stairs. His loss was about to become Tom Endicott's gain.

Business picked up as the morning wore on. About half the customers brought in some books to swap and stopped at the counter to dicker with Roxy. The rest went directly downstairs. No one said a word about Brahms—only one customer had even mentioned classical music. She was a saintly looking, white-haired piano teacher from the New England Conservatory—so she said—looking for an obscure collection of Chopin Etudes. Endicott was supposed to come up if he saw anything out of the ordinary in the basement. Maybe his nephew was concentrating on the nurse and forgetting business. Charlie thought, "Is it possible that I misread the situation. I wonder what's going on at Fletcher's?"

Just then Charlie heard a voice with a definite foreign accent say, in response to the usual question from Roxy, "Half cash and half swap." The accent sounded French but not the French that Charlie learned at Harvard. Charlie looked up. Roxy was giving the man her little speech about the swap coupons. This time she didn't completely succeed in screening the envelope delivery. Why was she wasting an envelope to give a customer a couple of coupons and some money?

Charlie took a more careful look at the man waiting at the counter. He wore a cloth golfing cap from the Bobby Jones era that covered most of his dark, greasy hair. Shaggy eyebrows, a full moustache, and a scar from a razor fight accented an olive-skinned complexion. Charlie guessed that he came from the Mediterranean coast of France. What had the man said? "Cash *and* swap?" What an unusual thing to say in response to Roxy's question. At least six others including that smasher of a nurse had said the same thing. This could be the gimmick to identify a person entitled to receive that week's drug supply. Collins' tale of Scarlotti's approach in Barney's Bookstore had conditioned him to believe that some reference to the composer of the mystery selection was necessary. When Scarlotti asked for a book about Chopin, he may well have alerted the gang that he was a fake. The envelope he had seen passed was too small to hold anything like a wholesale supply of drugs for a week. Still, it could hold a baggage check or directions as to where the pickup could be made.

The man said, "I'll come back to pick up some books when I have more time." He headed for the door.

Charlie went to the stairwell and flicked the light for the stairs off then on again. Roxy was looking at him curiously. Charlie said, "Tell my friend downstairs I just remembered something I have to do right away. I'll see him back at his apartment."

He left the store to follow the Frenchman.

✴   ✴   ✴   ✴

Downstairs, Tom Endicott had been happily engaged in the All-American sport of girl watching. The nurse was using a stepladder to reach books on the upper shelves. As she climbed up she displayed more than a flash of shapely leg. When the stairwell light went off and on again, she was at the top of the ladder and began to teeter.

"Help, please help!" she cried. By now the basement was nearly full of people, but Tom was clearly the only one close enough to take action in time. He dashed across to catch her as she fell. They both wound up on the floor in a heap. Fortunately for Tom he managed to land on top.

"Delightfully pneumatic!" he said.

"What did you say?" she asked in stunned disbelief.

"Delightfully pneumatic," he repeated. "It's a line from Huxley's *Brave New World*. It's a compliment, I assure you. Are you okay?" He gave her a hand to help her up.

"I'm afraid I've turned my ankle," she said, rubbing that attractive asset gingerly. "Could you possibly help me upstairs and get me a cab?"

"Certainly," said Tom. Old Charlie would have to look after himself. He couldn't desert a damsel in distress. There were three other young men looking on enviously. Any one of them would have been glad to take over for Tom. He ignored them.

"My name is Tom Endicott, a third-year law student." Well, he was almost a third-year law student.

"Not the Tom Endicott who shares an apartment on Inman Avenue? I've heard about the wild parties there. My roommates have been to a couple. The last time they didn't come home for two days."

"We don't deserve the notoriety," said Tom. "Don't believe everything you hear. Since it's your left ankle, put your left arm around my neck and lean on me. That should take the weight off it."

When they reached the sidewalk, Tom was amazed to see a police cruiser in the near foreground. A uniformed cop had a man leaning against the wall in the "frisk" position. Charlie Witherspoon was sitting on the sidewalk in a daze, rubbing his head, while a plainclothesman looked on. Just then an empty cab slowed at the nearest intersection. While Tom was watching Charlie and the police, the nurse hailed the cab and ran to catch it. Tom turned in time to see that she was running without any trace of a limp. She was in the cab and gone before Tom realized he hadn't even gotten her name.

Maybe she'd show up some time at one of their parties. Anyhow, he was having dinner with Tina tonight. He shouldn't even be thinking about strange females. He yanked himself back to the present and approached the group near the squad car. Collins, who had not met Tom, was about to tell him to shove off when Charlie interceded.

"It's all right, lieutenant. This is my nephew, Tom Endicott. He was in the bookstore with me, and it's his apartment Fisher was killed in."

"Is that any kind of recommendation?" asked Collins, looking around for suspicious characters. "Who is that crummy-looking broad in the doorway of the bookstore?" Roxy was taking in the scene with her gimlet eyes. She bent over as if to pick up something and then went back inside.

"That's Roxy, the owner. She's a holy terror. She's in this racket somehow, up to her scrawny neck. She's been handing out envelopes all morning to customers who say the right thing."

Collins held up a hand to shut him up in case the Frenchman could overhear. Fortunately, the cop had locked the suspect in the back of the squad car with the windows closed. "What was the right thing for the customers to say," continued Collins, "something about Brahms or that piece he wrote?" Collins seemed sure of the answer.

"That's what I was expecting," said Charlie. "I wasted most of the morning until the truth finally struck me. When a customer brings in books to swap, Roxy asks, 'Cash or swap?' To the few who reply 'Cash *and* swap,' she gives an envelope. I don't suppose you have a search warrant on you. I'd love to see what she has left in that desk of hers."

Collins looked shame-faced. "We've got a warrant for Fletcher's, but there's been no action there this morning except for an Episcopalian priest making a date with a choirgirl. By the time I could get one for this place, she'd have it cleaned out. Still, there's no harm in trying."

"Get your warrant," said Charlie, "but I doubt there will be anything more going on at Roxy's today." His sharp eyes had spotted the sign of the crab in yellow chalk on the sidewalk. "Look at that chalk mark right in front of the door to the bookstore. I'll bet anything incriminating has been locked in the safe or moved out the back door."

Collins moved closer to the door to inspect. He came back showing his disgust, heading for the cruiser radio.

"At least I'll get a video truck over here to take pitchers of any crumb who gets close enough to read that sign." The patrolman had been standing by patiently waiting for Collins to notice him.

"Okay, Anderson. What did you find on the Frog?"

Charlie winced at this display of bigotry, but he was beginning to get used to Collins' tendency to act and sound like Archie Bunker.

"A police thirty-eight—that's what he used to sap this gentleman with." Anderson pointed at Charlie. "I doubt that he has a permit for it."

"Probably not registered either," said Collins. "In this state that's a mandatory one-year jail sentence. No milk-toast of a judge can suspend the sentence, and he can't get time off for good behavior." Collins smiled as if he personally would enjoy every minute of the sentence.

"A wallet," continued Anderson, "with the usual stuff—fifty-six dollars in cash, two credit cards, and a driver's license."

"What's the spic's name?" asked Collins.

"What is he, French or Spanish?" said Charlie. "You can't have it both ways."

Collins ignored the interruption.

"Anton Benoit of Woonsocket, Rhode Island," said Anderson.

"There's quite a pocket of Canucks livin' in Woonsocket," said Collins. "That French-Canadian accent must have fooled you college boys," he said to Charlie and Tom.

Anderson had been saving the best for last. "And then there's this white envelope." He held it gingerly by one corner. "I haven't opened it yet."

"Good thinking, son. Proably just his prints and Roxy's, maybe not hers if she was being careful, but you never know. Get a plastic bag from the cruiser for it. We'll get the fingerprint boys at the station to open and test it." He turned to Charlie who was now on his feet and seemed hardly the worse for wear. "Witherspoon, maybe we should get a doctor to look at you. This area is lousy with hospitals. The nearest emergency room is within spitting distance."

"No thanks," said Charlie. "I was a medical student for two years, and some of my best friends are doctors. I know too much about emergency rooms. It's not that the interns who man them don't know their stuff. They're better in many ways than the older doctors many of whom are not up to date on the latest techniques and medicines. The problem is that the intern may have been on his feet for thirty-six hours or longer. I wouldn't trust him to give me an aspirin. Anyhow, I'm sure I'm okay—not even a concussion. The first blow glanced off my arm, and fortunately Anderson, here, was out of the squad car and had that junkie under control before he could hit me again."

"Your arm looks a bit beat up to me," said Collins. "I thought I told you not to try playing cops and robbers." The words sounded tough, but his tone was conciliatory. Collins was on the defensive since it was clear the police had been watching the wrong bookstore. They'd have had nothing to show for this day's work if Charlie and Tom hadn't done some sleuthing on their own.

"Lieutenant, I swear I was on my way to phone you. The nearest phone booth is in a drugstore halfway up the next block. I never got that far. Something I did inside the store must have tipped him off, or maybe Roxy signaled him somehow. I thought I'd lost him when he stepped out of an alley behind me. If a dog hadn't rattled an ashcan lid just then I wouldn't have seen him out of the corner of an eye and had time to throw up an arm to protect my head. Besides, Endicott here was supposed to be lending a hand. It turns out he was too busy trying to pick up a nurse to notice my signal. Isn't that about the size of it?" Charlie looked at Tom accusingly.

Tom Endicott looked sheepish. "I'll admit I was had. Just when you hit the light switch to signal me, she started losing her balance on a stepladder. It was like something out of a ballet. When I rushed over to help her, she fell on top of me and knocked me down. Then she claimed she'd sprained her ankle and wanted help getting upstairs. As soon as we made it to the street and I was distracted by you guys, she spotted a cab and ran for it like an Olympic sprinter. All I could see was her dust."

"Come to think of it," said Charlie, "she was one of those who said, 'Cash *and* swap' to Roxy. I'll bet she's got an envelope too, although I didn't see it being handed over. I suppose you've already made a date with her. At least we'll know her name and address."

Tom made a face. Then a thought occurred to him. "If Roxy slipped her the high sign, which seems likely, anything she told me would have been false."

"You amateurs are always making excuses," said Collins.

Across the street the video truck appeared and quickly pulled into a parking space just vacated by a station wagon. "Let's get out of here," said Collins. "The cruiser will scare away anyone thinking of dealing with Roxy. Just a minute, though; I've got one thing to do first." He quickly walked to the doorway of the bookstore to a place where he couldn't be seen from the inside. He pulled out his handkerchief, spat on it and carefully rubbed away the yellow chalk mark.

"Maybe she won't notice it's gone," he said as he climbed into the passenger side of the cruiser's front seat. Anderson took over the wheel. Collins cranked down the window on his side to say, "We want both of you back at the station to get a statement. It's not safe in the rear with the Frog there. The windows and doors open only from the outside, and there's bulletproof glass between the front and rear seats. Take a cab and the department will pick up the tab."

CHAPTER 18

▼

Charlie Witherspoon and Tom Endicott dictated their statements in Collins' office with occasional interruptions from Libertino, who had been called in because of the possible connection with the Fisher case. When they finished, Collins left the room briefly with the envelope they had found on Benoit.

Charlie and Tom decided to wait while the statements were being typed to avoid an extra trip the next day.

Collins came back with a metal key and dropped it on the top of his desk. "Go ahead, pick it up," he said. "We've drawn a blank on prints. It's too bad. The key is small, but big enough to take a thumbprint. The smooth surface of the key is ideal—not like the ribbed surface on a gun handle."

Libertino said, "I'm sure I've seen a key like that somewhere. I just can't remember where.

Witherspoon, who had done more traveling than anyone else in the room, spoke up, "I'm sure it's a storage locker key."

"Talk about a fuckin' needle in a fuckin' haystack," said Collins. "I'll bet there are more than 500 of those lousy lockers in Boston and Cambridge. Railroad stations, bus stations, airport terminals—there's even a set at the Park Street subway station."

"Harvard Square, too," said Tom, feeling that he'd been left out of the conversation.

"The point is," said Collins, "there's no number on the key. Even if we knew the number, there'd be a dozen places to try."

"I'm not so sure about that," said Charlie. "There may be no more than two companies serving the area, which would mean only one or two sets of numbers to worry about. One more point. This key has an opaque plastic coating of some type. I'll bet they dipped the key to hide the number and confuse people as to what the key was for. The dealer knows in advance what airport terminal or station is intended as his regular drop. He uses the right solvent, and the number reappears. My guess is that one of the ketones would work. Have you got any nail polish remover handy?"

Collins looked insulted at the question. "That'll be the day when you catch me painting my nails."

Libertino laughed. "Betty Jelinek has some. She's on the plainclothes detail we use in the park. She's quite a dish when she's all dolled up—likes to use bright red polish to match her lipstick. She looks frail, but I've seen her throw a 200-pound mugger over her shoulder. She's not a woman to mess around with—unless she asks you, of course."

Libertino left and came back shortly with a small bottle and a porcelain cup. "We have some plastic glasses, but I was afraid the nail polish remover might dissolve them."

"That would make a mess," said Charlie. He put the key in the bottom of the cup, pouring in just enough liquid to cover the key. The coating on the key dissolved, exposing bare metal. No numbers were visible.

"Shit!" said Collins.

"Keep your shirt on," said Charlie. "Let's turn the key over." He took a pencil from Collins' desk and flipped the key, holding the grip portion out of the liquid. The number 239 became visible.

Libertino slammed his fist down on the desk so hard the cup nearly overturned.

Charlie looked at him in amazement. "You're lucky you didn't break something."

Libertino said, "I'm a double-barreled stupid son of a bitch. I should have asked Grabowski one more question."

"What's that dumb Polack got to do with it?" asked Collins.

"He's a neighbor of mine, the one who called me about the mugging at South Station. You remember that black guy—Whitey Jones—the dealer who drove a purple Caddie. There was a gangland style execution a few days after the murder. His body was found in the trunk of a car near Porter Square."

"Yeah," said Collins. "The Gomez brothers lifted an attaché case from Whitey, a case with at least a cool hundred grand worth of pure horse."

"The point is," continued Libertino, "Whitey went right by a set of lockers coming out of South station before he ran into the Gomez boys. Grabowski told me Tones came out the Summer St. side of the station, near Atlantic Ave."

"Why wait until three a.m. to pick up something that valuable?" asked Charlie. "Wouldn't there be customers waiting for their fix on Saturday?"

"That's probably why he was killed," said Collins, "Either because of the delay or because he was stupid enough to let a couple of young Spiks take the stuff away from him. Whitey Jones was at least two levels above the ordinary pusher. The horse would be cut at each level. That takes time."

"Whitey had a reputation as a lady killer," said Libertino. "He was probably sidetracked by some dish after he picked up the key, perhaps on his way to South Station. The purple Cadillac was a powerful attraction."

Collins looked at his watch. "It's nearly two. I'm tempted to go over to South Station now—we'd at least find out whether this key fits one of the lockers. They may have cleaned it out by now. It depends on whether Roxy has warned them."

"She had no reason to connect the cruiser with the bookstore," said Charlie. "Some cruising cops stop to help a solid citizen who is being beaten up. That's all."

Collins hit his intercom switch. "Sergeant, see if Riley and Taylor are back from City Hall Plaza. They are? Send them into my office." He turned to talk to Libertino. "If we stake out the area, we may make jackasses out of ourselves. If ten men pick up attaché cases from those lockers, we haven't got enough manpower to tail them. Arresting them would make us look even sillier if it turns out there's nothing but business papers inside."

"It's not as bad as it looks," said Charlie. "As a lawyer, I'm practically never separated from my briefcase while traveling. I might check a suitcase with my clothes in a storage locker in the morning if I'm going out of town that evening from the same station. My briefcase almost always has papers in it that I'll need during the day. I think it would be highly unusual for a businessman to check his attaché case in one of those lockers."

Libertino was looking through the phone book. "I never realized there were so many Poles in the Boston area. Here it is: 'Walenty Grabowski.' May I use your phone, Bill?"

"Be my guest," said Collins.

Libertino dialed the number as soon as he got an outside dial tone. "Hello, Walenty. Glad I caught you at home. You remember the mugging victim you talked to a coupla weeks ago, after that delayed train trip from New York?"

"The short black guy, dressed to the nines, with a purple Caddie? Not likely I'd forget," said Walenty.

"Did you see him get off the train with the attaché case, the one the muggers made off with?"

"I'm not sure I did. Wait—it's coming back to me. I saw him for the first time near the storage lockers, the ones you pass just as you're leaving the station to go out on Atlantic Avenue. He was closing the locker with one hand and had the case in the other."

"Thank you very much, Walenty. We shouldn't have to bother you again." He turned to Collins. "Grabowski confirms that Whitey Jones took a case from a South Station locker just before he was mugged. We can guess why he was killed."

Collins nodded his head. "Like I said before, he made at least two mistakes. He should have picked up the case earlier when there were commuters in the station. That way he would have attracted less attention. Also, it would have been safer. Then he let himself get mugged and ripped off by two punks. His carelessness slowed down the distribution of that week's stuff and could have put the kibosh on the whole scheme. Let's hope it does. I'm worried that this afternoon's work may cause the ring to close down the bookstore method of distribution before we can put a finger on the ringleaders."

"Maybe not," said Charlie. "They may still think their code is secure. Tom and I could have just stumbled on Roxy's Bookswap. We did nothing in the store to behave other than ordinary customers. Also, there's a good chance the gang has found out that the police staked out the wrong store. These things have a way of getting around. Finally, the gang could change their code and go on using bookstores. There are too many of them for you to cover them all."

"You know how to cheer a guy up," said Collins. "Most of the stuff in the storage lockers has probably been picked up by now. What you say is a good reason for not arresting anyone at South Station—assuming anyone shows from now on. If someone does show, we'll let him make the pickup and tail him very carefully. He may lead us to one of the men at the top. In any case, if we don't blow it, they may try the locker stunt again next week."

Riley and Taylor appeared in the doorway. Riley said, "You wanted us?"

"Sorry to have wasted your time this morning, boys. By the way, Taylor, I want to talk to you about the shoeshine boy."

Taylor looked flabbergasted. "I don't understand," he said.

Collins laughed. "The next time you do something stupid, don't do it with an open mike on your walkie-talkie. Here's what I want you to do. This here's a key that may open a locker at South Station—number 239—try the set of lockers at the corner of Atlantic and Summer first, then the ones in the rest of the station. If you get the locker open and it's empty, you might as well go home, but call in first to give me the bad news. If there's an attaché case or anything else in the locker that might contain dope, leave it there, then put in enough coins to lock the locker again. Then one of you calls in while the other watches the locker. We don't want to miss this bugger again.

"What about backup?" asked Riley.

"Don't teach your grandmother to suck eggs," said Collins. "I'll arrange for an unmarked car to be at the Summer Street entrance to the station, close to the Atlantic Avenue intersection. You'll know the car by its XYZ plate. If the target comes out of the station and hails a cab, you pass the tail to the unmarked car. Touch your forehead twice to show when he's supposed to take over. I'd rather have the target get away than realize we're on his tail. Of course, it'll be your ass if he does get away."

"You can't win in this outfit," said Taylor. "What if he takes the subway?"

"Then one of you goes with him while the other calls in—as soon as he knows what direction he's going. Take one of those newfangled pen cameras with you. We'd like a picture of this guy if nothing else.

Charlie picked up the Yellow Pages section of the phone book from Collins' desk. There was something about the cover that was different from the book he had used in the public library.

Collins interrupted his train of thought by bellowing into his phone. "Lynch, get yourself the car with the XYZ plates and head for South Station. Pick up a partner first. Here's what I want you to do."

CHAPTER 19

▼

Riley sat on a raised chair getting his shoes shined while pretending to read a newspaper. Actually, he had been watching the locker across from him like a hawk ever since they found an attaché case inside. The case was of beautifully dressed calfskin with a combination lock. Riley had seen one just like it in the window of London Harness for 200 dollars. They hadn't tried to force the lock. The case had the feel of being full.

Riley had carefully paid in advance for his shine, explaining that he might have to leave in a hurry, perhaps with only one shoe done. His story was that a jealous husband was following him. The story sounded thin to him, but the shoeshine boy—why did he think of him as a boy when his gray hair proclaimed him to be in his sixties?—swallowed it whole.

The shoeshine boy gave him a conspiratorial grin. "I'll give you such a good shine, that husband'll never recconize ya."

Riley thought that least he'd be able to make a quick getaway. He remembered with embarrassment the last time he had a shoeshine while on a surveillance operation. The suspect or "tailee" had finished his meal much faster than Riley believed possible. The shine job was only half done. When Riley had tried to leap from his chair to run after the target, he'd found himself in the iron grip of the shoeshine boy. By the time Riley had been able to dig the money out of his wallet, he had completely lost the target. He'd been the butt of Collins' jokes for an entire year afterwards.

Taylor, too, was thinking about shoeshine boys and the way that kid had kicked him in the shins that morning. He was still sore about the twenty dollars.

Taylor was out on Summer Street in front of South Station. He spotted the unmarked car with the XYZ plates. He recognized the driver, Jimmy O'Hara, a cousin on the Boston police force. O'Hara was ready to move if Taylor gave him the high sign. Taylor paced the sidewalk, pretending a woman had stood him up.

A man approached the lockers from the ticket office and waiting room side. His turtleneck sweater and horn-rimmed glasses gave him the air of the academic, possibly an associate professor or a very young full professor. There was not a trace of gray in the hair that was styled fashionably long in soft waves, but still short enough to reveal part of the ears. He moved jerkily toward locker 239, checking the numbers as he went. Either he was not the man who put the case in the locker, or possibly he was just absent-minded. Taylor remembered the time he'd parked his car at Logan and couldn't remember where. It had taken him an hour to find it.

The professor took out a key, opened the locker door, and took out the case. He headed for Summer Street and the subway entrance without undue haste but as if he were going to an important faculty meeting and didn't want to be late. Riley was just getting out of the shoeshine chair and was able to follow unobtrusively. Out on the sidewalk he signaled Taylor who managed to take three shots with his pen camera as Turtleneck passed. Taylor followed both of them down under South Station until they were both on a car for Harvard Square. Then he ran back up the stair to get out in the open so that he could call Collins on his transceiver. The radio hadn't been built yet that could send or receive from South Station Under.

Turtleneck sat on the left side of the car with the case loosely between his feet. He showed no awareness of Riley's presence and never bothered to look at the case. Riley wondered how he could be so casual with a small fortune in drugs in his possession, particularly when thefts on the MTA were all too common. All the thief had to do was make his grab and leave the car just as the doors were closing. There would rarely be anyone on the platform to stop him. If there were anyone, he would be more likely to cheer the thief on than try to stop him. Riley stood near the rear of the car next to a door so that he could leave quickly if Turtleneck made his move—standard operating procedure.

At Washington Street about half the car emptied, headed for bargain basement shopping. A man with a Van Dyke beard got on and sat down next to Turtleneck. Van Dyke had the air of a London banker going to his job in the City by tube because his Rolls Royce had broken down. He too had an attaché case on the floor between his feet. Only later would Riley remember that the case was identical to the one Turtleneck had taken from the South Station locker. Riley had no reason then to be suspicious of Van Dyke. He'd taken one of the few vacant seats when he got on, and there had been no sign of any attempted communication between him and Turtleneck.

As the car approached Park Street Under, Van Dyke went through the motions of a man who has lost or misplaced something—he searched various pockets in vain. At Park Street he rose suddenly, turning his back to Riley and for a moment obscuring Riley's view of Turtleneck. Then Van Dyke picked up a case from the floor and exited by the nearest left-hand door. He crossed the platform and entered a car that was about to leave in the opposite direction.

After they left Charles Street, Turtleneck picked up his case from the floor and balanced it on his lap. When he opened the case, Riley could see that it was empty except for a paperback novel and a crumpled brown paper bag. The bag might still hold the remnants of his lunch but certainly not a fortune in heroin or cocaine.

Riley knew he'd been had—at least in the sense that he hadn't noticed the switch. On the other hand, if he had chased after Van Dyke, he probably would have lost him—the split-second timing in changing trains had been perfect—and he would have alerted Turtleneck to the tail. Riley could still follow him unobtrusively and keep on the good side of Collins. Maybe Collins would have the inspiration to get a man over to Harvard Square, after Park Street the busiest stop on the Red Line. In all probability, Turtleneck would get off there.

Turtleneck sat reading his paperback as if he didn't have a care in the world. He made no move to leave as the train stopped at Kendall and again at Central. Either he had decided that no one was following him or would try some trick at Harvard to flush any tail.

Harvard Square, then the terminus of the Red Line, had an abundance of exits. When the train pulled in, Turtleneck started briskly off toward the main exit which came up to street level in the center of the Square, right across from the Coop. Just as he got to the foot of the stairs, he did an abrupt about face. Then he headed for a rear exit that would bring him up on the north side of Mass. Ave. just outside the Yard.

Riley, who had been about ten yards behind him on the way to the main exit, nearly panicked at the maneuver. Then he saw Hennessey and stopped dead to look for something in his hip wallet just as Turtleneck passed going in the opposite direction. This was the signal for Hennessey to take over and to identify the target. Riley had to use all his willpower not to turn around to watch Hennessey and Turtleneck. He climbed the steps and headed north on the west side of Mass. Ave. He saw Turtleneck just ahead of him on the other side of the street, walking along the red brick wall that bordered Harvard Yard. Hennessey was a discreet distance behind him. Riley didn't give either of them a second glance. He turned left on Garden and found a sheltered spot near Christ's Church where Turtleneck couldn't see him. He pulled out his transceiver to report to Collins.

When Riley had finished, Collins said, "Good work, you guys; it almost makes up for the way you and Taylor botched things this morning at City Hall Plaza. I'll get an unmarked car over there to support Hennessey. Over and out."

*   *   *   *

Back in Central Square, John Rogers had joined the group in Collins' office. He inspected the prints of Turtleneck fresh from the police dark room.

"I think it's Fleming," he said. "There's something about the shape of the head and the nose. The hair's shorter than it was when I met him. I can see at least part of his ears in the picture; they were completely covered by his hair then. How did he move?"

"Short, sudden moves—like he had St. Vitus Dance," said Taylor.

"That fits," said Rogers.

"It doesn't get us much forrader," said Collins. "Hennessey just called in to say that he lost Turtleneck—or Fleming, if you like—at the Law School. Our man in the car didn't get there in time. Turtleneck ducked into the basement of Langdell Hall and disappeared."

"There's a men's room down there," said Charlie. "He could take off the sweater and glasses and leave them behind with the case. Even if he didn't change his appearance, there's an underground passage from Langdell to other Law School buildings. From that passage there are at least a dozen different exits he could have taken. You'd need an army to cover them all." Charlie changed the subject. "Did the search at Roxy's turn up anything?"

"I decided against asking for a warrant," said Collins. "A search would have been sure to put them off the bookstore method of distribution for next week. We also decided to play it safe with Benoit. At first I was tempted to get our friends in Boston to move him around from station to station to make it hard for the gang to get him released on bail. We've done just the opposite, made it easy for them. We even got the police chemist to paint the key with some black nail polish. The number is covered up again so the key looks just the way it did when we took it off the Frog. Now be has everything but his gun—we impounded that as evidence—and he's back on the street."

"This gang seems to have a safety net," said Charlie.

"I agree," said Collins. "The way I see it, the dealers are supposed to pick up their stuff in the morning—certainly no later than one p.m.—and pick up their dope by mid-afternoon. Somebody with duplicate keys checks the lockers in the late afternoon, just as they did with the locker at South Station today. If someone has missed a pickup, like the Canuck did today because he was in police custody, the gang takes the stuff back. After the bad experience with Whitey Jones, they won't take the chance that it will get in to the wrong hands."

"How is the stuff paid for?" asked Tom.

"That's been bugging me," said Collins. "In this business it's cash on the barrelhead, either in advance or when the goods are delivered. You guys didn't see any cash change hands this afternoon, did you?" His face lit up like a thousand-watt bulb as a sudden thought struck him. "Maybe the customer hid the money in a hollowed-out book he brought in to swap."

"I didn't always get a clear view of what Roxy was doing," said Charlie, "but I did see her leaf through most of the books to examine their condition. I'm sure I would have noticed any large wad of cash or a hollowed-out book. I heard her tell one customer that once she found a ten-dollar bill in a paperback that had been brought in to trade. Apparently it had been used as a bookmark. At least once I saw her take some pieces of paper—not money—out of a book somebody had brought in."

"What did she do with them?" asked Collins.

"I'm trying to concentrate," said Charlie. "I didn't attach any importance to the pieces of paper at the time. I was expecting drugs and money to change hands."

"I was going to ask you why you left this info out of your statement."

"It's coming back to me," said Charlie. "She put them in a drawer near the cash register."

"If they weren't money, why the hell would she save them?" asked Collins. "You'd think she'd hand them back to the customer or throw them in the waste basket."

"They might have been cashiers checks, payable to bearer," said Charlie. "As good as money, probably harder to trace than a certified check which would have to have Roxy's name on it."

"I remember something about cash transactions over a certain amount having to be reported to the federal government," said Tom.

"Right on!" said Charlie. "The threshold figure is 10,000 dollars. Then any cash transaction has to be reported by the bank to the Treasury Department. That would explain why there was more than one piece of paper. I'm not up on current prices for high-grade cocaine, but I know that $10,000 wouldn't be nearly enough to pay for an attaché case full. So the guy goes to as many banks as necessary to get the number of checks he wants in sums smaller than $10,000."

CHAPTER 20

▼

Tom Endicott and Tina Forbes lay on the king-size bed in Julie Everett's apartment, curled up together in happy exhaustion.

"I still don't understand it," said Tom, "how a girl with your talents could avoid getting mixed up with some man before now."

"I wish you'd learn to say 'woman'. 'Girl' somehow sounds adolescent. Anyway, I came awfully close my freshman year. There was this smooth character from Westfield, N.J.—played tennis for Princeton as I remember. He sent me this beautiful poem, handwritten as if he'd created it especially for me. The poem was so moving I'd have jumped into bed with him given the slightest opportunity. The next day after I received this tidbit in the mail, our English prof read the poem to the class: Elisabeth Barrett Browning's 'How do I Love Thee.'"

"At least he had good taste," said Tom, restraining the impulse to ask her how she could have made it all the way to Radcliffe without reading the poem before.

Tina sensed the question. "Somehow I missed out on poetry until I got to college. My parents thought I had the makings of a tennis champion. From the time I was seven I practiced at least four hours a day. I was very good, but I lacked the killer instinct. I was a junior in high school when I finally said the hell with it. I ditched tennis completely and concentrated on history, French, and Math. Otherwise I'd never have made it to Radcliffe."

"Thank God you did," said Tom, running a hand lightly over her thigh. "How did you deal with this Westfield character?"

"At the time I was so furious with Hugh that I didn't talk with him or answer his letters. Later I realized I over-reacted and was taking out my own stupidity on him. I convinced myself it was sweet of him to copy out the poem by hand when he could have sent me a photocopy."

Tom didn't agree, but he wasn't going to argue.

"What about you?" asked Tina. "What was your closest call?"

Tom wasn't sure he liked her assumption he had been a virgin until he met her. "It happened just before Christmas of my first year here. The woman who owned the apartment building—'Widder Brown' we called her after the old radio show—lived in the basement and acted as her own caretaker. She was built like a pro football defensive guard. I'd seen her move furniture it would take two men to handle. No one believed she had a real knockout of a daughter. I'm not sure I'd have joined the group if I'd known the daughter was going to be living in the basement, too. The Widder Brown wasn't too keen either about having her daughter move in. She knew something about the ways of law school students."

"What happened?" asked Tina.

"Rosemary—the daughter, that is—dropped out of college some place in the Midwest. She was only eighteen. Instead of being at the apartment only during vacations, when most of us would be away, too, she started living there full time. When I met her for the first time, I knew she'd be trouble. After dinner that night I called a council of war—sort of a firm meeting. I said I was no prude about what sort of sex life they wanted to have, but it would be a tragic mistake for any of us to get mixed up with Rosemary. The atmosphere was too charged, what with her living in the basement and her mother to reckon with, not to mention the fact that we were there to learn the law. Rosemary would be too much of a distraction. Everyone agreed with me—even Pete van Pelt, the most active woman chaser in the Northeast. I thought we had the problem under control."

"Oh dear," said Tina. "I wish could have began there to hear your Dutch uncle speech. I bet you sounded terribly smug."

"The irony of it all was that I was the first to get involved," said Tom.

"Just like the minister in the story by Somerset Maugham, you remember the man who tried to reform Sadie Thompson?"

"Unfortunately I never did get to sleep with her, although I sure as hell was given credit for it—maybe I should say blame instead of credit. The night before I went home for Christmas vacation, there was a big party at Hastings Hall, mostly law students and their wives or dates. Rosemary came with a third-year student who drank too much and passed out early in the evening. She asked me to rescue her as the only other person there she knew and could trust. I didn't get drunk but became relaxed enough to lose most of my inhibitions. When the party started to fade, we went with another couple to a nightspot in Boston. I discovered she wasn't as innocent as she seemed. She wanted me to take her to a hotel. I didn't have enough cash on me and no credit card. I knew what a razzing I would get if I took her back to the apartment. Even so, it was four in the morning when I finally got her home. Her mother was furious. As luck would have it, Pete van Pelt came in from a late date just in time to hear her bawling me out. He was really lying in wait for me when I finally came upstairs. He thought the whole thing was a tremendous joke; he flatly refused to believe the evening had been a completely innocent one. I knew the story would be all over Cambridge in the morning. Thank God Christmas vacation had started. There wouldn't be too many students around for him to tell. The whole thing stood a good chance of being forgotten by the time I came back after New Year's. When I did get back, I found that van Pelt, the old lecher, had entertained Rosemary in his room, while the Widder Brown thought her daughter was with me."

Tina was laughing so hard now she nearly fell out of bed.

Tom continued, "The worst part was the disillusionment. I'd more than half fallen for the little tramp, thinking she was a sweet young thing who needed to be protected from the van Pelts of this world."

CHAPTER 21

▼

Pete van Pelt was as good as his word. He picked up Charlie's *Golden Bough* volumes Saturday night on his way to a foreign flick at the Exeter. When Tom came back to his apartment Sunday morning just before noon to change his clothes, he found the books in a used liquor carton on top of his desk.

"They weigh a ton," said van Pelt. "I wonder when your uncle is going to find time to read all that crap."

"He's a confirmed bachelor without any woman in his life—at least at the moment. Reading and listening to music are his main forms of relaxation." Tom sat down at the desk, removed the books from the carton and arranged them in order. "That's strange," he said. "There are thirteen volumes—two copies of Volume One." As he picked up the duplicate volume to leaf through it, several pieces of paper fell to the floor. They were bank deposit slips, each from a different bank, totaling $36,000. He picked up the phone to call Charlie.

"I was just about to call you," said Charlie. "Did Pete pick up my books last night?"

"Yes. I think you'd better come over here to look at them."

"I've been thinking," said Charlie. "It's not very practical to take those twelve volumes back on the plane—awkward to get them to the airport, and they'll cost me a small fortune in excess baggage. You could ship them to me parcel post, book rate, or UPS and it would save me a lot of trouble and expense."

"I'd be glad to, but I still think you should come over right away to see what I found in one of the books." He explained about the two copies of volume one and the deposit slips.

"I'll call Lt. Collins," said Charlie. "I think he'll want us to meet him in his office. In any case, I'll come by in a cab as soon as I've talked to him. Put the duplicate volume and the slips in a plastic bag without touching them any more than you have to."

Tom said, "I've been on this case longer than you have. Please give me credit for some sense."

Collins was not in his office—not surprising for a Sunday, and Sergeant Hennessey refused to give out his phone number. He did, however, take Charlie's number and promised to pass it on, saying, "The lieutenant will call you if he thinks it's important enough."

Collins was reading the funnies and about to open his first beer of the day when Hennessey called. "Damn it!" he said. "Why can't it wait until Monday?" He took down Charlie's number, though.

After wrestling with his conscience for a moment, he made the call. When Charlie had completed his report, Collins said, "Pick up Endicott, the book and the slips and meet me at my office pronto. Maybe I'll be able to get back home before the Red Sox game starts. They're playing the White Sox in Chicago, which gives me an extra hour. By the way, bring both copies of the first volume of that set. I want to see what the differences are, if any. Tell him to hold everything by the edges and wrap it up. We still may get some useful prints.

Charlie didn't tell him he'd already given instructions. He also doubted that a bank deposit slip would take a good print, especially the carbon copy. The paper wasn't glossy enough.

In his office, Collins used a pair of tweezers to get the deposit slips out of the plastic bag, then took the slips out to the copying machine in the hall. He told Hennessey to deliver the books and the originals of the slips to the lab. He knew that the one man on duty might not be able to get to them for a while. Then he took the copies back into his office to join Endicott and Witherspoon.

The three of them looked at the copies of the deposit slips spread out on Collins' desk. Harvard Trust, First National, State Street, and Shawmut were the banks involved. The name of the account, "Crimson Liquors," was the same in each case. The amounts deposited were in the low eight thousands and high nine thousands.

"Neat but not gaudy," said Charlie. "This explains how the dealers paid for their dope. I assume the total of $36,000 would be about right for the quantity of high grade heroin that would fit comfortably into an attaché case."

"That's a good ballpark figure," said Collins. "Of course the stuff would be cut four or five times in the process of getting to the user."

"I should have thought of this sooner," said Charlie, shaking his head ruefully. "I have to admire the beauty and simplicity of it. A person using cash to make a deposit doesn't have to sign anything or even identify himself. If he knows the account number and name, he's home free. I'll bet most banks would furnish the account number to a would-be depositor. It's not as if they were giving out the number of a Swiss account. Also each of the amounts is less than $10,000 so the bank doesn't have to report the transaction. What about this Crimson Liquors—do you know anything about them?"

Collins said, "They're the exclusive distributor for some fancy brands of whiskey, gin, vodka, and wine. They've got a big warehouse in North Cambridge. As far as I know, they're completely legit. I'll get someone on it as soon as I can. Monday we'll lean on the bankers and maybe learn something from them."

Charlie said, "Tom and I will look at their corporate papers on file at the State House. I know we can find out who their officers and directors are as well as the original incorporators. Stock ownership will be more difficult. The stock may be privately held or in the names of nominees."

"Let me see if I unnerstan' how they work their system," said Collins. "The dealer makes deposits in special accounts in three or four different banks some time during the day on Friday. That night he listens to the mystery tune on radio to find out what bookstore to go to on Saturday. Saturday morning he swaps the deposit slips for a locker key and picks up the stuff. How does he know which set of lockers to go to?"

Charlie was smart enough to sense that Collins wanted to answer his own question.

Collins' brows furrowed in deep thought. "There may be something about the key to tell him, its shape or color coding. Maybe each dealer has a set of lockers assigned to him in advance."

"Why do they need more than one location for lockers?" asked Tom.

"I think this is a big operation," said Collins. "In some ways it would be easier to plant everything at one location, but it would be more likely to attract attention. Putting twenty-five cases into one set of lockers would stick out like a sore thumb unless different people did it at different times. In this type of game, you want to keep down the number of people involved. Also, you might not find enough vacant lockers."

"We'll find out next Friday and Saturday whether they'll give this distribution method another whirl," said Charlie. "Unless you need me for something more at the moment, I'm late for a lunch date with Professor Rosenblatt."

CHAPTER 22

▼

Monday promised to be a real stinker, one of those late spring days that is hotter than any day of the summer. The wind was blowing from the southwest, bringing with it all of the heat and humidity of Houston and New Orleans. Rosie had postponed his return to New York because the Dean wanted a written report on the true-false test incident. Rosie wanted to talk to Emily Quince before putting the finishing touches on the report. Emily would be the ideal person to type the final report. While a lot of rumors were still flying about, only a handful of people knew what Rosie knew. It was better to keep it that way as much as possible.

Emily called Sunday evening to say that her father's condition was steadily improving. She'd been able to find a full-time housekeeper at a reasonable price: a widow who could cook. He was home now. The only problem was that the widow might try to latch on to Mr. Quince, a risk that Emily was prepared to take. Emily was going to Italy in July, and nothing was going to stop her now. She'd be in Rosie's office Monday and Tuesday to clear up any loose ends then off on Wednesday to Milan, Florence, and Rome.

By agreement with Sgt. Libertino, Rosie told Emily that the sergeant wanted to talk to her about Fisher, in the hope that she could shed some light on the motive and who his enemies were. Libertino agreed to let Rosie sit in on the meeting on the understanding that Rosie would keep his mouth shut unless asked a specific question. Of course, after the sergeant left, he planned to ask some questions of his own if the ground hadn't already been covered.

With graduation over, the law school building had a deserted, ghostly air even though there was some business going on. The faculty was still busy grading exams for the first and second-year students and planning next year's courses. The sergeant, Rosie, and Emily Quince were seated in the same conference room where the law students had been questioned about the evidence exam.

"Did Fisher have any enemies?" asked Libertino.

"I can't think of anyone who hated him enough to kill him," said Emily.

"What about the students he tutored who failed to make the grade?"

"Some of them did complain, but Lawrence's policy was to cheerfully refund half the tutoring fees if the student flunked. He felt this was good advertising. He told them in advance that he couldn't promise success, but the refund guarantee made the students feel they'd pass the exams. In fact, Lawrence was a remarkable teacher. His students did very well. Some of them have gone on to law review."

"How did the faculty get along with him?"

"Most of them thought he was a good thing. If the student could be salvaged, the law school gained as well. A few professors were opposed to any form of private tutoring on the theory that it helped a lazy student with money to get by, resulting in a second or third-class lawyer."

"How do you know what the faculty thought?" asked Libertino.

"Sometimes Professor Thorndike would repeat his colleagues' comments. Professor Thorndike is my regular boss—I'll go back to work for him in the fall. Most of my information, though, comes from the secretarial grapevine. Not much in this law school goes on without our knowing it, sometimes when most of the faculty is in the dark. I can't wait to see my friends and catch up on the gossip."

Libertino said, "Could Fisher have got hold of the answers to the true-false part of the evidence exam?

"Impossible," Emily said. "Professor Rosenblatt held on to the answers himself. Even I have never seen them." She gave Rosie a look of reproach.

"I understand that Fisher was a skilled lawyer," said Libertino. "Experienced in the law of evidence as a trial lawyer."

"That's true, from what I've heard," said Emily.

"So, all he needed was access to the questions. He could come up with the answers without any help."

Emily paled. "I don't understand what's been going on. I wasn't aware of any problem with that exam."

"Fisher was peddling the answers to students during the week before the exam. We're sure he was trying to sell even though we can't prove that any students bought."

Emily said, "I took the test to the printers myself. It was never out of my hands."

"Was Fisher with you when you went to the printers?"

A look of consternation came over Emily's face. "As a matter of fact, I ran into him right outside this office building. We stopped for a cup of coffee in the Square." She blushed. "I did leave him for a few minutes to powder my nose. I don't see how he would have had time to copy anything. No problem if the answers had been available, but the questions were long and complicated. He'd have needed a flash to photograph them, wouldn't he?"

"With today's miniature cameras and fast film he could have made copies without anyone noticing. Even if someone did see what he was doing, why butt in?"

"Sergeant, if he did steal that test, I'll kill him." She gasped as she suddenly realized what she had just said. "I swear I didn't know about the possibility until just now. When I left for New Hampshire to take care of my father, I hadn't heard a word about the exam answers being for sale or anything about cheating."

Libertino looked at Rosie. "What about the anonymous phone call you had the morning before the exam, the caller who claimed the test answers had been sold?"

Rosie said, "I always take my own calls unless I have a visitor or am trying to really concentrate on something. Then I tell Emily in advance."

"Can't she listen in on your phone simply by picking up hers and pushing the right button?"

"She can, but she never does unless I ask her to." Rosie was a knight in shining armor defending the honor of his secretary. "In any case, there's an audible click when someone picks up the extension. I know there was no click during that call."

"Where were you the evening before the exam was given?" Libertino asked Emily.

"I had dinner with Lawrence, the last time I saw him. It was an early night because he had a tutoring session at nine. I went home to write some letters I had been putting off."

Libertino was brutal. "We know that he showed up at a party about 9:30; it must have been a short tutoring session."

"The student may not have shown up," said Emily. "It wouldn't have been the first time."

"You seem to be good at making excuses for Fisher," said Libertino.

"I guess I am," said Emily. "I suppose you know something about us?"

"I know that you visited him regularly in prison and that you'd been engaged to be married for five years. That's along time in anyone's book. Did you know that he was stringing you along, making out with other women?"

"I know that once in a while he was unfaithful," said Emily. "I suppose I was a fool to put up with him, but these little affairs never lasted. I know that if they did, I would have heard. There are always a few friends who can't wait to tell you that kind of bad news."

"Can you prove that you didn't go out again that evening?" asked Libertino. "I'm inclined to believe that you had nothing to do with Fisher's death, but in this business I can't go by my feelings alone."

"I don't see how I can prove it, Sergeant. I live by myself in a studio apartment close to the Radcliffe dorms. No one came to see me that evening. I'm sorry it wasn't a Monday night when our bridge group meets."

"Did you make or receive any telephone calls?"

"Not that I recall."

"What about the hospital in New Hampshire? When did they call to tell you about your father's illness?"

"Not until Friday morning when they caught me at the office. Wait a minute. I did call the library Thursday night to renew a book that was due that day."

"What time was that?" asked Libertino politely, thinking that the time would be too early and that in any case she could have called from a phone booth.

"About 8:45," said Emily. "The library closes at nine. I went out to the kitchen to check a date on the calendar and saw the book next to the phone. I put it there as a reminder."

"Fisher was killed between three and five a.m.," said Libertino.

"Why didn't you say so in the first place?" said Emily. "All of the tenants in our building are women, except one—a Caspar Milquetoast type who's sure he's going to be robbed and killed by an intruder. As a result, you wouldn't believe the security measures. There are steel bars on all of the windows and at least one deadbolt and chain latch on all of the outside doors. After 6 p.m., the front door is the only way that you can get in with a key. At midnight the superintendent, who lives in the basement, shoots the bolts and chains the front door. Then you can't get in unless someone lets you in. The Super doesn't like his beauty sleep disturbed."

"That's something that can be easily checked. I'll get a man over there this afternoon or tomorrow morning. Are you going to stay put for a while?"

"I'm leaving for an Italian vacation Wednesday evening. It would be nice to know I'm in the clear when I board the plane. You might need some wild horses to drag me off it."

"I really hope you won't have to postpone your vacation," said Libertino. "The north of Italy is delightful this time of year. Rome and Naples are too hot for me."

CHAPTER 23

▼

That same morning, Tom met Charlie at the Commander for breakfast. He wore slacks, dress shirt, tie, and an olive linen sport jacket instead of his usual T-shirt and jeans. He had considered wearing his only suit and decided against it. The wind had changed to the northwest bringing in cool air from Canada with enough sunshine to keep the temperature in the seventies.

"This sure beats my home cooking," said Tom, as he polished off a half-grapefruit, two fried eggs with bacon, followed by pancakes with real maple syrup, all washed down with three cups of black coffee. "Where do we start on this Crimson Liquors outfit?"

"Let's go up to my room," said Charlie. "I think a telephone call is in order before we spend any time at the State House. It's occurred to me that Crimson Liquors may not be a corporation at all. There may be no record at the Secretary of State's office, except possibly a trade name registration."

A short time later Charlie hung up the phone in his room and said to Tom, "It would have been a wasted trip if we'd gone to the State House. There's no corporation under that name."

"What's the alternative?" asked Tom. "Could it be an individual or partnership doing business under that name?"

"You have learned something here," said Charlie. "If the owner or owners have had good legal advice, they've filed a statement with the clerk at the Cambridge City Hall. That's just off Mass. Avenue in Central Square. Let's get the show on the road."

The assistant clerk, an attractive brunette in her mid-thirties, was friendly and cooperative. She found the Crimson Liquors' filing promptly. "We get a lot of these," she said. "The law requires that the statement be signed in person in front of the clerk and that identification be shown. I remember the person who brought this in because it seemed strange that a relatively young woman could be the owner of a sizable outfit like Crimson Liquors. If you've ever been up there, you'd know that their warehouse is almost as big as the Sears store in Porter Square."

"Can you describe the woman?" asked Charlie.

The clerk looked at the date on the statement. "It was more than a year ago when she came in, sir. She was very attractive, about my height—five-six, that is—and no more than thirty. I don't remember the color of her eyes or hair, although I do remember thinking at the time that it wasn't her own hair. Some of the wigs these days are so good, it's difficult to tell."

"What about her clothes?" asked Tom. In his experience, women remembered clothes if nothing else.

"She had on a tailored gray suit with a Paisley scarf and a pair of alligator shoes I'd kill for. The perfume was expensive, too."

Charlie looked at the form again to be sure he had it right. "Could I have a picture of this please? I'd be glad to pay the usual fee."

The clerk took the form to the back of the room where a Xerox machine was humming away.

"It says Jane Ransome of Wendell Street in Cambridge," Charlie said to Tom. "That's near the Law School. It used to be mostly rooming houses, although sometimes a group of students would manage to rent an entire house."

"The neighborhood hasn't changed," said Tom.

The woman returned with a copy of the form.

Charlie asked her, "Can we be sure that the name she used here is her real one?"

"I always ask to see a driver's license, passport or some I.D. with a picture on it. Unless the picture is a reasonable likeness, we have the right to insist on more evidence. It's our responsibility to protect the public she's doing business with."

"I wish all public servants were as conscientious as you are," said Charlie, betting that a fake driver's license could be had in Cambridge for a small fee. As they left the building he said to Tom, "Since we're in the area, let's call on Lt. Collins and bring him up to date."

They found Collins sitting at his desk, chewing his fingernails. He was a man suffering the agonies of indecision. "I can't make up my mind what to do about those deposit slips you brought in yesterday. What's going to happen when the gang finds out they're missing? I'm afraid we've blown it."

Charlie said, "I think it would be worse for me to take them back to Roxy. It would be difficult to be nonchalant about $38,000 in deposit slips. It's apparently her job to check the deposit slips before handing over the storage locker key. If she's sure she did that, she may not worry about what happened to the slips, or if she does worry, forget what book they came in or what she did with them."

"Won't the syndicate insist that she turn over enough slips to account for the amount of horse dished out?" asked Collins.

"Not necessarily," said Charlie. "It depends on how high up she is in this gang and other factors. What's the date today?"

Collins looked at his desk calendar. "The third of June," he said. "What gives about the date, anyhow?"

"The deposit slips are really only a form of insurance today in case the bank records get destroyed or erased. Before the day of computers, the customer got only a stamped copy of his deposit slip. After the bank was closed to the public, some clerk would take the deposit slip and enter the transaction manually in the bank records. There was always the possibility of getting the money in the wrong account or entering the wrong amount. With a computer in the picture, the so-called deposit slip is actually a print-out of the entry in the bank records that the teller has made by computer, showing the account number, the amount deposited and the new total in the account."

Tom said, "I heard about a clever crook who took deposit slips coded with his account number and put them on top of the regular deposit forms in the lobby of the bank. At the end of the day, more than $10,000 had been credited to his account."

"That couldn't happen in most banks today where the teller punches in the account number and gets a display of the account name and current balance."

"You still haven't told me why you asked about the date," said Collins.

"Because the banks should shortly be sending out statements for the month of May. Once Crimson Liquors has its statements, showing the proper deposits, the slips can be thrown away."

"The other thing that's been bugging me is how to approach the banks without tipping off Crimson Liquors. These banks know which side their bread is buttered on. I'll bet they'll tell their customer we've been asking questions."

"I think I know how to kill two birds with one stone,' said Charlie. "But first, let us fill you in on what we found out over at City Hall." He handed Collins the Doing Business statement and repeated their conversation with the clerk.

When he mentioned the woman wearing a Paisley scarf, Collins said, "That description rings a bell somehow, but I can't put a name to the woman. I'm sure it wasn't Ransome, though. Damn it! I know it'll come to me later. I'll probably wake up out of a sound sleep at three tomorrow morning with the name on my lips."

Charlie said, "I've got a friend at Splithair, Cavil & Quibble, the Boston law firm that represents one of the banks involved here. If I put the matter to him properly, I'm sure we can work something out. These banks have a public relations problem. Quite apart from the legalities, if it ever became public knowledge that the banks had aided a drug operation—no matter how unwittingly—the fat would be in the fire."

*   *   *   *

Fifteen minutes later, Reginald Quibble, a son of the founder and a partner in the firm, was in Collins' office.

"The president of the bank and I met at lunch the other day just to discuss this subject—the use of banks by drug syndicates to launder their money and for other nefarious purposes." Quibble said. "He's very much concerned about the matter and not just on moral grounds. He's scared to death there will be more federal regulation in this field. His theory is that if the banks do a good voluntary job of policing, they can escape a lot of red tape. Did you know that in Miami some drug dealers bring in cash by the carton to be counted? Sometimes they bring in so much it isn't even counted, merely separated into denominations and weighed."

"What about the requirement that cash transactions of $10,000 or more be reported to the Treasury?" asked Charlie.

"Treasury doesn't have the manpower to enforce that regulation when there are widespread violations, as in the Miami area. The banks ignore the regulation even if they get caught—which is rarely. The fine is like a slap on the wrist, peanuts compared to the amount of money they earn from their laundering operations. I talked to Chet—the president of the bank that is—before I came over here. He is checking out the Crimson Liquors account on the computer display screen in his office. Let's give him a call. What do you want to know?"

"The account volume," said Collins, "and who gets payments from them."

"It would be interesting," said Charlie, "to compare the volume of anonymous cash deposits with the total deposits in the form of ordinary checks from their retail liquor store customers. Also ask if there have been any inquiries about this deposit slip. He handed Quibble a copy of one of the slips on Collins' desk."

Quibble made notes then picked up the phone. After a brisk conversation with Chet, he reported, "Crimson Liquors had May deposits totaling 1.1 million dollars; checks drawn on the account totaled slightly less."

"That's only one account," said Collins. "There are accounts at three other banks, at least three."

"Reg, can you put the arm on your counterparts to get the same information from the other banks?" asked Charlie.

"I'll sure try," said Quibble. "I think they'll cooperate. Let me go back to my office to make some phone calls. I have to be there to take a call from Washington at eleven. Can you let me have copies of the other deposit slips? Incidentally, on the other questions you asked, Chet's administrative assistant is working on them. She'll be in touch with you soon."

$$*\qquad*\qquad*\qquad*$$

When the group reassembled in Collins' office after lunch, they had computer printouts from all four banks. A financial picture for Crimson Liquors began to emerge. Total deposits for the month of May were 4.5 million dollars, two million of this from anonymous cash deposits, the balance from 100 different retail liquor stores. Withdrawals totaled 4.4 million, all to well-known distilleries or large regional super distributors.

"How are the people at the top getting their cut?" asked Collins.

"Certainly not by check," said Charlie. "They don't want anything with their names on it to make it harder for you and the IRS to catch up with them. They may have another bank account from which they make cash payments."

"Perhaps they take it out in trade," said Tom. "So many cases of pure malt Scotch at a time."

"Out of the mouths of babes," said Charlie. "You just may be on to something. Let's look at the print out of sales to Crimson Liquors' retail customers. Which one's the largest?"

It didn't take them long to discover that Bebidas Alcoholicas Alvarez of San Juan, Puerto Rico, was by far the largest customer. The volume of its purchases in May was equal to that of all other purchases combined.

"That rings an alarm bell," said Charlie. "From a geographic point of view, it doesn't make sense to service a retail store in San Juan from a wholesale warehouse in Cambridge. If the selling price is unrealistically low, it's a diversion of profits from Crimson Liquors to this Alvarez outfit in Puerto Rico."

Tom spoke up. "From what John Rogers tells me, and he's already taken one advanced tax course, the tax bite in Puerto Rico is less than it is here."

"Good point," said Charlie. "It so happens that I know the District Director of the IRS in Boston. He used to be with their Chicago office—a tough man but a reasonable one. May I use your phone, Lieutenant? I'll need to look up his number. Wait a minute, hand me the Yellow Pages, too. The last time I was in here I noticed your Yellow Pages had a different cover."

"Different than what?" asked Collins.

"Different from the cover on the Yellow Pages at the Boston Public Library. This says 'July, 1969'. That's the latest, isn't it?"

"I think so," said Collins. "The new one must be in the pipeline."

Charlie turned to the Bookstores-Retail section. Barney's was the seventh store listed. Some store ahead of it in the listing must have gone out of business since the 1968 Yellow Pages edition was issued. He showed Collins where Barney's now stood—number seven.

"I think it was just coincidence that the Chopin mazurka that John Rogers played a week ago last Friday night was in B flat. The opus number, seven, was the real key, just like the Brahms piece last Friday night, opus 120, meant Roxy's place. It proves you were right about Barney's, though. Some of the dealers must have showed up there until the warning sign was chalked on the sidewalk."

Collins' expression changed from irritation to sheer smugness. "I tole ya. I got a nose for crime. I could smell something wrong with that store. There's no substitute for experience."

Charlie had found the number he wanted in the U.S. Government listings, got an outside line, and dialed the number.

"Internal Revenue Service."

"Let me speak to the District Director, please, Charles Witherspoon from Chicago calling." Charlie didn't say where he was calling from. He found that people tended to pay more attention to a long-distance call.

"Just a moment, sir."

Charlie had to repeat his name to a secretary. She put him on hold to check with her boss, and then said, "Mr. Harris is coming to the phone."

"Charlie, you old legal eagle, what brings you back to the scene of your many crimes?" Bill Harris was familiar with Charlie's eleven-year stretch at Harvard and seized every opportunity to rib him about it.

"It started out as my tenth reunion at the Law School," said Charlie, "but for once in your life, you're partly right. It seems to be crime that's keeping me here. Have you ever audited Crimson Liquors, a wholesaler located in North Cambridge?"

"Today seems to be the day for coincidences," said Harris. "I've just finished reviewing the file on Crimson liquors—an audit for the tax year 1968. The file is still on my desk. You know that a tax return and the audit file are confidential information. I can get my ass in a sling if I violate a taxpayer's rights."

"I'm sitting in the office of Lieutenant Collins, Cambridge police," said Charlie. "In a small way, I'm helping him to investigate a major drug distribution scheme in this area. Cash from the downstream activities seems to be funneling into Crimson Liquors. It's a sole proprietorship owned by a woman name Jane Ransome. We can't believe she is one of the principals. We suspect the profits are being siphoned off to a Puerto Rican retailer. We're trying to find out who the ringleaders are."

"Do you know the name of the retailer?" asked Harris.

"Bebidas Alcoholicas Alvarez," said Charlie.

"Since you know practically everything we know, I see no reason not to confirm that you're on the right track. In 1968, Crimson Liquors had gross sales of over three million dollars, but a net profit of only twenty-five thousand. Much too low for any reasonably well run operation."

"What about a salary for Mrs. Ransome?" asked Charlie. "If I remember my tax law correctly, since she is the sole owner of an unincorporated business, she'd be taxed on the profits whether she paid herself a salary or not."

"True," said Harris, "but she did pay herself a salary, too. That way she could get additional tax benefit from a percentage of her salary being paid into a retirement plan."

"How did she get the capital to start the business?" asked Charlie. "That large warehouse in North Cambridge must have cost several million."

"That was one of the things that caught our eye during the audit," said Harris. "A Miami bank advanced the money at an extremely favorable rate, and the terms of the loan require only interest payments for the first five years."

"So most of the profits of the Massachusetts operation are being diverted to Puerto Rico?" said Charlie.

"Exactly," said Harris. "We've been through the records here with a fine-toothed comb. The invoices to Puerto Rico show a selling price averaging less than five per cent over cost."

"You'd think it wouldn't be practical to ship the liquor from a distillery in Kentucky, say, to a warehouse in Massachusetts, and then reship it to Puerto Rico."

"You're quite right. It wouldn't be practical. The shipping and handling costs would kill you. The distillery ships it directly to San Juan, but bills Crimson Liquors—their customer—rather than the Alvarez outfit in San Juan. They call it a drop shipment. I'd expect you to be aware of such things with an MBA from Harvard among your trophies."

"They don't teach you that at Harvard,"said Charlie. "That's something you learn in the school of hard knocks. When I got my MBA back in the fifties, I was offered a job with one of the Fortune 500 companies. I expected to move into the executive suite—that's the way it would work today in most companies. Then they wanted me to open up a new sales territory in Montana on an expense allowance of twelve dollars a day. I'd have had to stay in sleazy hotels and eat the cheapest thing on the menu. That's when I decided to go to medical school and maintain myself in the style to which I had become accustomed."

Collins gave Charlie a glare of disapproval at the digression.

"How did Mrs. Ransome explain the low prices?" asked Charlie.

"She claimed they were some kind of a quantity discount. At one stage in our questioning she threw up her hands, fluttered her eyelashes and played to perfection the role of the helpless female. Her performance was just a shade too good to be true. She's about as helpless as an 800-pound gorilla."

"You say you don't know who owns the San Juan company?" asked Charlie.

"It's a corporation set up by a local law firm, three of whose associates show up as the incorporators. All the shares are in bearer form. We'd love to find out who owns them. If the holders are U.S. citizens, as we suspect, we could really make things hot for them—criminal charges and all that. The problem is, for some purposes, Puerto Rico is part of the United States, and for other purposes it's not. Even if these guys are Puerto Ricans, the income is really U.S. source, and they should be paying taxes at our higher rates. It would be more difficult to prove, harder to make a criminal case stick, and they might not have assets in this country we could seize."

"What about Mrs. Ransome?" asked Charlie.

"Oh, she'd be in hot water, too, if we could prove a connection between her and the owners of Alvarez Liquors. If you are able to get a warrant to search her home or apartment, look for instructions coming from Puerto Rico. She'd be too smart to keep them at Crimson Liquors."

"Wouldn't she be too smart to keep them any place?" asked Charlie. "I should think she get her instructions by phone in a coded message. If she did get written orders, wouldn't she destroy them?"

Harris said, "Our experience is that criminals and tax cheats do keep careful records, but in a separate set of books. They need the records so they can divide the spoils evenly and settle arguments. Keep us informed if you find anything."

"Thanks, Bill. We certainly will," said Charlie and hung up.

Collins said, "I'm planning to put a tail on the Ransome dame, three of our best men. She won't know that anyone's watching her. I don't see what else we can do until Thursday when Rogers finds out what the mystery tune for this week is, that is if they don't junk the system in the meantime."

"Even if they were planning to change the system," said Charlie, "I bet it would take them more than a week to work out the details and get the word out."

"They coulda had a fall-back plan from the start," said Collins. "I got respect for the mother fuckers behind this operation. They got brains up to a tall indian's asshole."

CHAPTER 24

▼

Tom Endicott's summer job didn't start until the beginning of the third week in June when the Boston law firm that had hired him for their training program started its vacation schedule. He'd be picking up part of the slack left by a young associate taking his first vacation. Tom had been warned that he'd be more trouble than he was worth and that he'd spend most of his time in the remotest recesses of the library doing legal research. The rest of his time would be spent on odd jobs such as taking notarized papers to the State House to have the Secretary of State certify that the notary really was a notary in good standing, then taking the certificate to a foreign consulate to have it legalized. The problem was that some of the consulates were open only on alternate Thursdays between three and four p.m., and then only if the day was not a national holiday of either country or the consul's birthday.

Because Tom knew he was in for a busy summer, he was determined to make the most of his remaining free time. Monday night he and Tina dragged Julie Everett's color TV into the bedroom, planning to watch a late movie. Halfway through the movie they both became disgusted with both the acting and the plot, and one thing led to another. When they finished, Tom barely had the strength to turn off the television and crawl back into bed.

✳   ✳   ✳   ✳

The next morning, Tom was thankful he hadn't arranged to meet Charlie until 10:30. He had time for a leisurely breakfast with Tina. Thank God she was a bacon and eggs type. For most of the past year at the Inman Avenue apartment Tom's practice had been to drink a quick cup of black coffee and run to avoid being late for class. He sometimes missed even that if Pete van Pelt forgot to take his turn making the coffee. He chuckled when he thought of the time Pete had climbed into a complete stranger's car with a half-grapefruit and a piece of toast. His own car had been in the shop and he had been expecting a friend to be parked outside waiting to pick him up.

"Do you want to come along with us?" Tom said to Tina. "Charlie and I plan to check out Barney's Bookstore. From what Collins tells us there's a great collection of secondhand books."

"Does the lieutenant know what you're up to?" asked Tina.

"We haven't consulted him so he can't tell us to stay away. Neither of us has been in the store before. There's no reason why we should alarm him. We really are going there just to look at books."

"I'm not that interested," said Tina.

"You might find something in your field at a discount," said Tom.

"I've already bought three fat books I'm supposed to read before classes start again for me on the fifteenth," said Tina. She was going to summer school to catch up because she had suddenly decided to change her major, a difficult decision in April of her junior year. "I'd better stay here and get started on the reading. It's important for me to conserve energy. I've been getting too much exercise recently."

*   *   *   *

When Tom and Charlie got to Barney's, they found Dapper Dan Callahan just letting somebody out through the fire exit. All they saw was a glimpse of a gray skirt. Callahan then became deeply involved with an old timer looking for Kenneth Roberts novels. Considering the fact that it was a Tuesday morning and that graduation was over, Tom and Charlie were not surprised to find the place otherwise deserted.

Tom headed for the paperbacks. It was his lucky day. He found a book he had read half of in a ski lodge and had been looking for ever since—a bittersweet novel of the forties, *The Second Happiest Day*, by John Phillips, J.P. Marquand's son. Then he stumbled on three Penguin versions of Margery Allingham's detective stories, books he'd never read before because they could not be sold new in the U.S. for copyright reasons. Albert Campion was one of his favorite detectives. He also found a hard cover copy of Sayers' *Murder Must Advertise*.

Charlie was indulging in nostalgia. He remembered spending a month with his grandparents on Long Island as a twelve-year old while his parents were off on a European junket. In the attic of the sprawling Easthampton house he'd found *Graustark*, a sentimental romance about a small European principality that had completely entranced him. Until now he had put the experience out of his mind as boyish folly. Now he was dying to read the book again. Barney's had a first edition, published in 1901 as well as two sequels, also first editions. The stories were dated and corny, and probably the first editions were of little value. Nevertheless, Charlie was delighted.

On the way out Tom sensed a hostile stare from Callahan. Callahan had been checking the price on *Murder Must Advertise* when Tom saw someone he knew passing by on the sidewalk. It was Taylor, one of Collins plainclothes detectives. When Tom felt the hostility, he looked back quickly to find only congeniality, Dapper Dan all smiles and Irish blarney. "I'm sure you'll enjoy those books, sir. They're old favorites of mine."

Outside the weather had changed abruptly from bright sunshine to a mass of cumulonimbus clouds, threatening a thunderstorm. Tom asked Charlie, "Did you see the owner giving me a dirty look? I was watching that detective of Collins pass the front of the store so I didn't see anything myself, but I sure as hell felt it. I don't remember ever seeing the man before, yet there's something vaguely familiar about him."

"I'm sorry," said Charlie. "I didn't notice. I was halfway through the first chapter of my book."

At the corner newsstand they ran into Taylor, who had been waiting for them. "You didn't see a woman in there, did you?" he asked. "A good-looker wearing a tailored gray suit and a scarf over her hair?"

"We did see a woman leaving by the emergency exit, just as we came in," said Charlie. "She was already most of the way out the door so that all we saw was a flash of gray skirt and a mighty trim ankle. You're supposed to be watching Jane Ransome, aren't you?"

"If that's not who she is, Collins will have us back pounding a beat," said Taylor. "We shot some film of her this morning coming out of Crimson Liquors, but there hasn't been time to get it developed. Riley and I tailed her all morning, with Hennessey helping in an unmarked car. We worked in shifts and changed our clothes around from time to time to keep her from getting suspicious—little things like reversing a topcoat, changing a hat, putting on specs."

Charlie thought that such tactics would certainly make him suspicious.

Taylor continued, "When she went into Barney's, I tipped off Riley to watch the back. Collins warned us there was a fire exit. Riley probably hasn't had a chance to use his walkie-talkie to let me know he's picked her up."

*   *   *   *

Inside Barney's, Dapper Dan was deep in thought.

The good news from Jane Ransome was the decision of the IRS not to pursue its tax deficiency assessment after a lengthy audit. They were home free unless one of the people in the know informed on them, and Callahan had seen to it that such people were very few and well compensated. Callahan and his two partners each had millions salted away in Bahamian banks. He and Jane were ready to turn over the operation to the Nardinis and leave the country after Saturday's shipment.

The bad news was the appearance in his bookstore of that law student, Tom Endicott. Endicott might remember him from the party at the Inman Avenue apartment the night Fisher was killed. Still, Endicott had shown no sign of recognition. Callahan couldn't place the man with Endicott although he looked like a blood relation. He decided not to take any action for the time being. Saturday night they'd be out of it. In the meantime he wouldn't take any unnecessary risks. He might have been better off if he'd worn his turtleneck outfit that night at the party.

CHAPTER 25

▼

Joe Libertino, reading the autopsy report on Lawrence Fisher for the first time, nearly lost his temper. The report had arrived the day before, a full ten days after Fisher's death. Because he had more important things to do and because he was sure of what would be in the report, Joe had put off reading it until today, Tuesday. According to the report, analysis of the stomach contents showed enough chloral hydrate to cause a man to lose consciousness. Damn it to hell! Knockout drops, the old-fashioned Mickey Finn. Libertino started looking for a scapegoat and called the medical examiner's office. The line was busy. Somebody, he thought, must have slipped the Mickey into Fisher's drink at the party. That meant it was an inside job. He finally got through to the M.E.'s office.

"Get me Dr. Donahue, please."

"Donahue here. What can I do for you?"

"Donahue, the question is what are you trying to do *to* me, not *for* me."

"Oh, Joe Libertino, I thought I recognized your voice. Which *corpus delicti* are you calling about?"

"Lawrence Fisher. You remember, the disbarred lawyer who was killed roughly ten days ago. You examined the body yourself at the scene. Now I find out from the autopsy report he was given a Mickey, knockout drops to you. You're probably too young to know what Mickey is."

"Look, Sergeant. I told you at the time, the man was suffocated with a pillow or something like a pillow. That still stands."

"Couldn't he have smothered himself if he was unconscious from the chloroform?"

"No way. He collapsed about 11 p.m., right. He'd been covered only with a sheet—too porous to shut off the air supply. Anyhow, the time of death was four or five hours later. The effects of the chloroform in that size dose would have been largely dissipated by then. Besides, there were signs of a struggle, abrasions on his face where he turned it trying to avoid the pillow."

"You could have called me," said Libertino, backing off a bit on his search for a scapegoat.

"You don't seem to have any idea what our workload is," said Donahue. "Analysis of the stomach contents is routine in a homicide case, but unless we mark the bottle 'urgent,' it usually takes about a week. When the cause of death is obvious, as it was here, we don't give the analysis any special priority."

"Thanks for the explanation," said Libertino, realizing that the real scapegoat was himself. He should have insisted on a prompt analysis of the stomach contents.

He went across the hall to bring Collins up to date on developments. "Once the drug angle came up and it looked like Fisher was killed by the syndicate, I assumed it was an outside job."

"Whaddya mean, 'outside'?" asked Collins.

"My theory was some hired killer followed Fisher to Inman Avenue, to the party, and waited for him to come out, planning to kill him on the street when it was dark and deserted. When the party shut down and Fisher still hadn't come out, the killer acted. He waited until all the lights were out, let himself in the apartment—none of those doors are ever properly locked and did the job."

"I'm right with ya," said Collins. "With a Mickey Finn in the picture, it's clear that the killer must have joined the party. That narrows the field." Collins got excited. "It also means they wouldn't have used a hired killer. He would have stuck out like a sore thumb at the party."

Libertino wasn't so sure. Some of the law students he'd seen could easily pass for gangsters, except they didn't dress as well.

Collins continued, "One of the top men in the syndicate—somebody who looked like a professor and who could mix with that crowd of students—decided to take on the contract himself."

Libertino thought the theory unlikely, but he knew he had to proceed with caution once Collins had the bit in his teeth. "That's worth following up," he said.

Collins shifted gears. "Taylor called in to report the Ransome dame showed up at Barney's this morning. Left by the rear exit. Good thing I warned Taylor and Riley about that fire door. Callahan may be our man. He taught at a ritzy boys school. He could easily mix with those Harvard types."

"Have you got a picture of Callahan?"

"There's one in the file. Pete Sullivan took a candid shot of him when he was in here the other day. We got him in to look at the film of the traffic outside Barney's the day that Scarlotti was in there—a week ago last Saturday. We also have a picture of Ms. Ransome in the works. Riley took it this morning as she was coming out of Crimson Liquors. He called in and we got a cruiser to pick up the film clip."

Collins picked up his phone. "Collins here. Howya coming with the film clip Riley sent in this morning, just an hour ago? All set. Great, can you send someone up with it pronto?" As Collins put down the phone another thought struck him. "I knew it would come to me if I didn't try to force it. Paisley, that's the kind of scarf that blond wore into Barney's. She's the one Jack Boyle said was as thick as thieves with Callahan."

He picked up the phone again. "Pete. Bill Collins. You remember the film of Barney's Bookstore you ran for me about ten days ago?"

"You mean the one with the chalked sign of the crab on the sidewalk? I sure do."

"What I want is a print of that blond in the gray suit—the one with the Paisley scarf, the babe I thought made the chalk mark. Can you get it up here fast?"

A short while later, Collins and Libertino were comparing photographs of the two women.

"I think you're right," said Libertino. "They're the same woman. The only difference is hair color and that's easy to change with dye or a wig."

Collins had found the picture of Callahan in the file along with the shots of Turtleneck taken at South Station.

Libertino examined them closely. "Suppose Callahan puts on a wig, a turtleneck sweater, and horn-rimmed glasses anytime be wants a different identity—Fleming, for example. Suppose Fisher is close enough to the truth to be a threat to the drug operation. Callahan hears that Fisher is going to the Inman Avenue party—a mob scene where no one will ask for an invitation. He grabs the opportunity."

"Why doesn't he do it in his Fleming disguise?" asked Collins.

"He knows that John Rogers lives in the downstairs apartment and is almost certain to be at the party. An encounter with him could be awkward. Besides, Fisher might be put on his guard if he saw Fleming. After all, he introduced Fleming to Rogers."

"What about the voice? That's hard to disguise," said Collins.

"Callahan doesn't have to talk to Fisher, just get close enough to drop the stuff in his drink. It would have been an easy thing to do in the confusion of that party. You have no idea, Bill, how many people were milling around in that small apartment. All Callahan would have to do is pass his hand over Fisher's glass and squeeze a palmed eyedropper."

"If he was going to slip him a Mickey, why not poison him and be done with it instead of using only knockout drops?" asked Collins.

"A quick poison like cyanide would bring the police down on the place like a ton of bricks. A slow poison could backfire. Someone might get him medical attention in time."

"I'll buy your theory," said Collins. "If Fleming with his sweater, wig and glasses shows up at the party, someone is sure to remember he was there even if Rogers or Fisher doesn't blow his cover. Callahan as himself is what I would call ordinary."

"What if Callahan noticed Endicott or Witherspoon this morning at Barney's?" asked Libertino. "Especially Endicott. He was one of the hosts, he was there the entire evening."

"Damn it!" said Collins. "Why should I have to act as a nursemaid for those legal eagles? After last Saturday you'd think they'd have enough sense to stay away from bookstores."

"I think we should put a man on Endicott for the rest of the week," said Libertino. "Maybe one on Witherspoon, too. At least we're up to full strength this week and crime so far is a bit slack." He knocked on Collins' desk superstitiously. "I'll leave a message at the Commander at also at Endicott's apartment. We'll convince them to join up so that one man can do the job."

The phone on Collins' desk rang. It was the sergeant on radio duty. "Lieutenant, I have Riley on the transceiver. I'll patch you in as usual."

"Riley here, outside Crimson Liquors. Subject has returned to her office. Taylor's watching the front of the building, Hennessey the back in his car. I'd sell my soul for something to eat right now. Over."

Collins said, "Eat first, then get your ass over to Mass. General. Find out what you can about Michelle Colbert, a nurse there. Get pix if you can. I'll call someone in personnel to grease the skids for you. Over."

"Roger, wilco, over and out."

Collins looked at his watch. "I better haul ass myself or I'll be late for the monthly meeting with my Boston counterpart and the feds. We can use all the help we can get. Will you call the personnel director at MGH for me?"

"Sure thing," said Libertino. "After all, it's part of a homicide investigation."

*   *   *   *

On their way back from Barney's to Harvard Square, Tom suggested they go to a soup and sandwich place that specialized in bean soups. Charlie ordered a black bean soup with sherry and a ham and Swiss on pumpernickel and then went to the phone booth. He called the mail desk at the Commander to check on messages.

"Only one call, Mr. Witherspoon, from a Sgt. Libertino. He said it was urgent."

Charlie dialed the Cambridge police station. "Sgt. Libertino, please, Charles Witherspoon calling." There was a short delay.

"Witherspoon, we got reason to believe you and Endicott may be in danger. Where are you calling from?" asked Libertino.

"A small restaurant called The Beanery, near Harvard Square."

"I know it," said Libertino. "I'm assigning a man to watch the two of you. It would be a help if you could team up, even sleep in the same room through Saturday at least. If you and Endicott will drop by after lunch, I'll explain. We want you to look at some pictures, too."

When Charlie reported this conversation to Tom, Tom said, "Why don't you stay at the apartment? Pete van Pelt is home for the rest of this week, maybe Monday and Tuesday, too. You'll save on hotel bills and breakfast enough to take me out to dinner."

At the station, Libertino showed them the candid shot of Callahan that Sullivan had taken.

"That's the guy who runs the bookstore we were in this morning," said Charlie. "Barney's on Mass. Avenue about half way to Porter Square."

"Have you ever seen him before, either of you?" asked Libertino.

"I don't think so," said Charlie. "I'm sure I'd remember that face. There's something Machiavellian about it."

"He was at the party we gave to celebrate the end of our exams—the night Fisher was killed. As I remember he didn't stay long. He may have left before you arrived, Charlie," said Tom.

"That may explain the dirty look you thought he gave you in the bookstore," said Charlie.

"We think he may dress up as Fleming to do his dirty work," said Libertino, "including Fisher's murder. The autopsy report shows someone gave Fisher knockout drops, a form of chloroform."

"All I can do is identify Callahan as one of 150 people who came to our party. There's no way to his knowledge that I could connect him with Fisher."

"Wait a minute," said Libertino. "I've got two other pictures to show you. He handed over the candid of Jane Ransome coming out of Crimson Liquors and the blow-up of the still frame from the movie taken outside Barney's.

"That's the nurse who tricked me at Roxy's last Saturday, the one who pretended to sprain her ankle. I'd know her anywhere," said Tom.

"We know she's been in to talk to Callahan this morning. All they need to do is put two and two together, and you become a real threat to their operation. Mind you, we don't want the police protection to be too obvious. We hope they go ahead with a bookstore distribution of the locker keys at least one more time.'

"In short, you want us to be tethered goats," said Charlie.

"Something like that," said Libertino. "Occasionally lawyers can serve a useful purpose in this world."

CHAPTER 26

▼

Callahan was having a meeting of his own with his two partners in crime. He had picked one of the bays in the parking garage underneath the Boston Common as the site. It was ideal because the multiple entrances and exits made surveillance difficult. It was impossible to bug and out of the sight of prying eyes. None of them had driven there because they couldn't count on finding a parking place these days. Callahan had accumulated seventy-five tickets for illegal parking in Boston. He couldn't risk leaving his car on the street, especially in a no-parking zone or he might find someone waiting to arrest him when he returned, a Denver boot, or both.

Callahan's partners were the Nardini brothers, Giuseppe and Giovanni. Both from Milan originally, they looked and talked more like respectable Italian businessmen than gangsters. They had financed the warehouse for Crimson Liquors—as well as provided working capital—all through a Miami bank.

"You think it's safe, one more time, to use a bookstore for passing out the keys?" asked Giuseppe.

"Not to worry," said Callahan. "The police don't know what they're doing. They staked out Fletcher's at Government Center last Saturday when all of the action was at Roxy's"

"What about the arrest of Benoit?" asked Giovanni. "Doesn't that show the police are on the right track, finally?"

"I talked to Benoit last Saturday night," said Callahan. "We were able to spring him quickly through a tame judge. The police found nothing incriminating on him except the gun. They paid no attention to the locker key. It was still covered with lacquer so the number was invisible. Even if they'd found the number, they'd have had no idea where to look."

"Why was Benoit arrested?"

"He pushed the panic button and attacked the man following him with the butt of his gun, trying only to knock him out. He thought the man was a plain-clothesman after the locker key. According to Roxy, the man was a lawyer in town for his class reunion. It was just a coincidence that he came out of the store after Benoit did."

Giovanni said, "If Benoit weren't our sister's son, he'd be in cement overshoes by now. As it is, we're moving him to the Montreal territory to keep him out of jail on the gun charge."

"Why did Roxy put the crab sign out?" asked Giuseppe.

"She was just playing it safe when she saw the cruiser pick up Benoit. If the cops had known about Roxy's, they would have sent an unmarked car. It was Benoit's bad luck that a cruiser happened by. When Roxy checked her records, she found that every key had been picked up."

"Has any thing else happened we should know about?" asked Giovanni. "We've come this far by playing it safe."

Callahan hesitated. They didn't know how close Fisher had come to the truth or his part in Fisher's death. Callahan had never read *Murder Must Advertise*. He thought of Endicott as a threat only in connection with the murder; he had no reason to believe Endicott knew anything about the drug racket.

Finally, Callahan said, "We are planning to watch our step. We'll use Barney's this Saturday to pass out the keys, with Jane in charge. She's done it before and she's smart enough not to make any mistakes. I won't be there. I'll be laying a false trail over in Boston. If anyone wants to follow me, I'll lead him a merry chase on the MTA. We really have no alternative. You gentlemen are taking over complete control of the operation next week. I suppose your system, whatever it is, isn't in place and ready to use yet."

The Nardini brothers nodded. Giovanni spoke, "It will take us a week more to add the finishing touches and get the word out. We won't go into the details except to say that partial instructions for the following week will be in this week's envelope with the key. Since you're getting out, the less you know about the new system, the better."

Callahan agreed. When the Nardini brothers first tried to take over the territory there had been real danger of open warfare. Callahan asked for a meeting and convinced them that he was almost ready to quit. He proposed a transition partnership with financial help from the Nardinis and the understanding that he could name the day when he wanted to get out and that he would be left completely alone when he retired.

CHAPTER 27

▼

When Collins arrived at his office Tuesday morning, he found Riley there waiting for him, a Cheshire cat grin on his face.

"What have you done to look so goddamned pleased with yourself?" asked Collins.

"I went to Massachusetts General like you said and got a picture of that nurse, Michelle Colbert. They let me have a spare print from her personnel file. She played the lead in a musical the hospital staff put on and they took some pictures for publicity."

Collins studied the photograph. "Close but no seegar, I'd say. Looks like she might be Ransome's sister, though."

"That's what I thought," said Riley. "I asked the personnel manager what she had on Jane Ransome. It turns out she was a nurse there until about five years ago. There was a picture in her file but no spare. I'm sure it's the woman from Crimson Liquors we've been following. Until she married a guy named Ransome, her name was Jeanne Colbert—Michelle's sister. At the time of her marriage she started using the name Jane. Then when her husband died, more than four years ago, she quit her nursing job. I gather it didn't pay very well."

"That's about when Crimson Liquors started doing business, in a much smaller building," said Collins. "Nice work asking those questions about Ransome. Maybe you've got more brains than I've been giving you credit for."

Riley thought wistfully about sergeant's stripes.

"Do the sisters live together?" asked Collins.

"No. Colbert shares an apartment with two other nurses on Blossom Street, just a stone's throw from the hospital. Ransome had a small apartment built into one corner of the Crimson Liquors' building when it was enlarged."

"See if Libertino is in. Tell him to get his ass over here—I mean, ask him if he'll join us." Collins remembered that Homicide rated a lieutenant in charge. Libertino had been the number two man in that department until Chapman was killed in the line of duty. All that Libertino needed now was a halfway decent score on the lieutenant's exam he had taken a month ago. With his veteran's preference, he'd be a shoo-in.

"I was on my way to see you," said Libertino, coming through the doorway with Riley in tow. "Witherspoon and Endicott got the message and stopped in yesterday afternoon while you were over in Boston. Endicott made Callahan. He was definitely at the law students' party. Endicott also surprised us with an ident of Ransome as the nurse at Roxy's last Saturday. You remember the woman who made a horse's ass out of him?"

"I didn't get a good look at her," said Collins. "All I remember is a white uniform getting in to a cab."

"We've got Lynch watching Witherspoon and Endicott. It turns out we can get by with one man because the subjects are being cooperative. Witherspoon has moved into the apartment, and Lynch has got a place to sleep on a daybed in the hallway just outside their bedroom."

"Isn't there a back door to that apartment?" asked Collins.

"Sure, but it's got a good deadbolt and chain. Anyone coming in either door would have to pass Lynch in the hallway to get at either bedroom."

"Have you got a man on Callahan yet?" asked Collins. "We could switch the team we got on Ransome. Now that we got her connected with Callahan, she's not so important."

"I wanted to check with you first," said Libertino. "Callahan—if he really is Turtleneck or Fleming, like we think—is a much more difficult person to follow than Ransome, and he's much more likely to spot the tail."

"I know," said Collins. "Remember that maneuver at the foot of the Harvard MTA stairs, the about-face that nearly caught Riley here with his pants down, not to mention the switcheroo of the case at Park Street? I don't want to scare him off. If we're lucky, we can wrap things up this Saturday."

"What about going for a search warrant, maybe an arrest warrant, too. I did some checking on Callahan yesterday. He lives by himself in an apartment near Porter Square. The building super there has a pedigree. He was in Walpole for a five to seven year stretch for armed robbery. He sold a sob story to the parole board, so he's out for the time being. All we need to mention to him is parole violation and he'll play ball."

"Whadya got in mind?" asked Collins.

"We'll search his apartment Saturday morning while he's busy at Barney's," said Libertino. "That's the biggest day of the week for the bookstore. Even if he somehow finds out that we've made the search, it'll be too late to call off the drug dealing. If we can get an arrest warrant we may decide to pull him in after the search so he can't alert his buddies."

"When do we pick up the dealers," asked Collins, "As they're taking the stuff out of the lockers? We're going to look pretty stupid if we arrest some Harvard type lawyer with a case full of legal papers. Shit! We don't even know which sets of lockers to stake out. It would take a small army of men to follow each of the slobs from the bookstore—assuming we know the right bookstore to watch."

"I think there's a way we can kill two birds with one stone," said Libertino. "Riley, can you tell me exactly what Turtleneck did last Saturday when he picked up the attaché case at South Station? Think carefully now. Every detail is important."

Riley closed his eyes and concentrated, recreating the scene at the lockers. As a trained observer, he had often used this trick before. "As he approached the lockers, he looked at the key in his hand, comparing its number with the numbers on the lockers. When he got to the right locker, he stopped, put the key in the lock, turned it and opened the door. He took the case out and put it on the floor. Then he took some coins from his pocket, put them in the slot, turned the key, took it out and put it in his pocket."

Libertino smiled. This was what he had been hoping for.

"What!" said Collins. "The stupid bastid pays good money to lock an empty locker?"

"Not so stupid when you think about it," said Libertino. "I think the stuff is put in the lockers some time during the day on Friday, when there are a lot of commuters or air travelers milling around. What a mess it would be if all the lockers happened to be full."

Collins said, "You mean, they're reserving the lockers for later use?"

"Something like that," said Libertino. "I talked to the local manager of Atlantic Locker Co. yesterday. They have concessions at North Station, South Station, and the bus terminals. They collect the coins from the lockers once a week—twice a week during the summer tourist season. If there's no money in a locker's coin box, they use a master key to open it and remove the contents, which they hold for the balance of thirty days as required by law. As long as there's some money there, they leave the locker alone."

"Don't tell me they use the same lockers every week," said Collins. "That way the dealer could cheat too easily—just hold on to his key and use it again the following week without paying."

"That possibility occurred to me, too," said Libertino. "I'm sure they stagger it so the same locker is used only every other week or every third week and not by the same dealer. Removing the key also takes care of another problem."

"What's that?"

"You remember how we removed the lacquer from the key of Benoit's to reveal the number?"

"Yeah. Witherspoon poured some nail polish remover into a coffee mug."

"I can't see a dealer doing that—too messy, and unnecessary. All you need to do is rub the handle portion of the key with a rag dipped in the solvent. Anyhow, either way the key would look strange smeared because of the solvent and the lacquer."

"I'm with you," said Collins. "The locker is kept for later use by removing the key. Otherwise someone else might use the locker, notice the smear on the key and start asking questions. The dealer turns in the key to the syndicate the next Saturday along with the deposit slips."

"That's my guess," said Libertino.

"What about the set of books Witherspoon bought, the extra volume one that had deposit slips in it? He didn't find no key."

"Roxy might have put the key away then got distracted before she could take care of the slips. Or the dealer could have been a first-time buyer. That way there'd be no key to return until the following week."

"You see what this means?" asked Collins.

"I think so," said Libertino. "We borrow the master key from the locker company. It's even possible the stationmaster has one, in case of emergencies. Friday night, when every thing is quiet, we open the lockers and note the numbers and locations of the ones with cases in them."

"If they use the same type of case they did the last time, it's certainly distinctive," said Riley.

Libertino continued. "This way we find out which locations have loaded lockers, and we don't waste men where they're not needed."

"A stakeout of three men starting at ten Saturday morning should do it," said Collins, "I mean three men at each location, of course. Even from a distance they can see the man they want, relocking an empty box. When a dealer picks up a case, one of our men can follow him out of the locker area before arresting him. That way we won't tip off the others."

"We'll need a Paddy Wagon hidden on a side street to take care of the perpetrators so our man can get back to the locker area." Libertino was furiously making notes. Then another thought occurred to him. "We don't really need to know which bookstore they're going to use," he said.

"You may be right," said Collins, "but I still wanna know if they call Rogers on Thursday. If they don't call him, it may mean they've worked out some new system that doesn't involve lockers."

"Assuming we get the tip on the bookstore, do we stake it out or leave it alone?" asked Libertino.

"Leave it alone, except maybe for a camera truck out front. This time we ought to get a real rogues' gallery."

"Maybe we should have a trial run at those lockers," said Libertino.

"Whaddya mean?" asked Collins.

"Inspect the lockers as soon as we can make arrangements, tomorrow morning perhaps. If our theory's right"—Libertino was being generous with the 'our'—"we'll find something like fifty locked, empty lockers in a minimum of three locations. Checking for locked, empty lockers is a damn sight easier than looking at an attaché case and trying to decide whether it's like the one Benoit was supposed to pick up. Only two men got a close look at that case, anyhow."

"You prolly got a point," said Collins. "There's no reason why the cases should be the same, unless they bought them wholesale or stole them from a warehouse. How do we do this trial run?"

"From what the locker company manager told me, his is the only company serving the Boston area. That means only one master key and maybe some uniforms if the guys that collect the coins wear uniforms. They do their job on Fridays. If we can get at it tomorrow there's no chance of running in to the regular crew. Maybe we'll get lucky. If we find the locked, empty lockers are only in two or three locations, we can skip the early Friday morning search completely. Some wino might notice and get the word back to Fleming."

"It could avoid anudder problem," said Collins. "I'm sure our boys are honest. Still it could be a terrible temptation—even for an honest cop—to open up one of those lockers at two a.m. with nobody else around and find a case loaded with coke or horse that could be sold on the street for more than he could make on the force in ten years. Give me the name of the locker company manager. I'll set the thing up for Hennessey and Sullivan to do tomorrow. They're already clued in to what's going on."

CHAPTER 28

▼

On Thursday afternoon, John Rogers sat by the telephone in the kitchen of the downstairs apartment with Charlie Witherspoon seated across the table from him. Looking out the window he could see children playing hopscotch on the sidewalk, taking advantage of the first halfway decent day they had had since Monday. Rogers was hoping the phone would not ring. When it did, he was surprised to hear a woman's voice.

"Mr. Rogers?" she inquired.

"Yes. John Rogers speaking."

"Chopin's Mazurka Number 7 in F Minor, opus 7," said the voice without any preliminary. "Have you got it right?"

Rogers wrote down the selection then repeated it over the phone. The woman hung up.

Charlie said, "It really is Barney's Bookstore this time. Callahan must be sure it's safe to do business as usual this Saturday, or maybe he's feels safer if he's minding the store himself." He picked up the phone to call Libertino.

"I'll want an affidavit from Rogers," said Libertino. "It may help us get the warrants. Incidentally, we'd like you down at the station Saturday morning around eleven—we'll call to when we're ready. Judging from past experience, I'll be glad to have your help in interpreting what we find. There's sure to be some legal or tax angle."

"Thanks," said Charlie. "I've seen so much of this play I wouldn't want to miss the final curtain." He turned to Rogers. "Isn't that mazurka the same selection you played before?"

"No," said Rogers. "It's another mazurka from the same opus. Thank God, this is the last time I'll have to do this. I'll tell you one thing. I'm not going to have a cup of coffee anywhere near the turntable tomorrow night. I may even pick up a spare just in case something happens to the radio station's copy. I'm still sore in some places from that beating two weeks ago."

Charlie picked up the phone again to call his law firm in Chicago collect. While they were tracking down John Conover he talked to his secretary to let her know of his impending return. Finally, a flustered Conover came on the line.

"I'm late for a regional meeting of the Yale Alumni Council," said Conover. "I haven't time to say more than hello and goodbye."

"That should be enough time," said Charlie. "I expect to be back in the office Monday morning. If there's any change, I'll call you at home over the weekend."

"We'll be glad to have you back," said Conover. "Be sure it's in one piece. See you Monday."

*   *   *   *

That evening, five of them played poker under the fluorescent light in the kitchen of the upstairs apartment—Endicott, Witherspoon, Flaherty, Rogers and Lynch, the police watchdog. Lynch was having an incredible run of luck. On the last hand—the fourth round of a jacks-to-open progressive series—Tom looked at three queens and bet ten dollars. Witherspoon and Lynch stayed; the others folded.

Charlie drew one card in an effort to improve his jacks and nines, and Bill Lynch also took one card. Tom, the dealer, took two.

Lynch is trying to fill a straight or flush, thought Charlie as he tucked a third jack into his hand.

When Tom checked, it was apparent he hadn't improved his openers. Charlie bet the limit. Lynch raised. After three successive raises, with Tom folding early, Charlie decided the policeman couldn't afford to lose any more and merely called him. Lynch laid down four bullets and a deuce and swept up the pot.

"Are you getting paid overtime for this watchdog detail?" asked Charlie.

"You bet your ass," said Lynch, counting his chips. "I seem to be more than 300 dollars ahead for the evening."

"According to the best legal authority, you should turn over your winnings to the department," said Charlie.

"If I'd lost the money, I'd have a fat chance of getting it out of the department. I'd like to see Collins' face if I asked him for it."

CHAPTER 29

▼

Friday morning at the station, Bill Collins brought Joe Libertino up to date.

Joe had spent the past two days in Washington attending an FBI seminar. "You'd be amazed how they're using computers these days, Bill. Any crook with a distinctive MO hasn't a chance now against the computer, so long as the locals remember to send the data in. Where do we stand on the lockers?"

"Hennessey and Sullivan wrapped it up for us. It took them most of the day Wednesday checking out all the lockers in the area. We're in luck. We got only three places to watch Saddiday—North Station, South Station and the Greyhound Terminal. Boston is providin' unmarked vans to use as Paddy wagons."

"What about the search warrant for Callahan?" asked Libertino.

"You got everything you asked for, includin' the right to search Crimson Liquors. Want any of my boys widya tomorrow?"

"I got a problem," said Libertino. "Callahan should be out of there by nine to go to his bookstore. Technically I should serve the warrant on him as the guy who rents the apartment, but we don't want to tip him off until we get some more hard evidence."

"What about a little snooping in advance?"

"Exactly what I've got in mind, and I think I've figured out a way to do it. The Super there tells me that Callahan's lease is up the first of September. He hasn't renewed it so the landlord has the right to show the place to prospective tenants. The Super lets me in after Callahan leaves and goes about his business. I take Sullivan with me—he's actually looking for an apartment—along with a good camera and some fast film. He takes pictures of anything that looks even vaguely incriminating. We bring it back with us to show you and Witherspoon. Later, we serve the warrant on Callahan when he's back in the apartment and pick up the originals."

"You got somebody set up to develop the film for you?" asked Collins.

"Sullivan's an old pro. He knows his way around the police dark room with his eyes shut; a good thing, too."

*   *   *   *

At the main office of the Harvard Trust Company, Callahan was cleaning out his safe deposit box: $10,000 in cash, his birth certificate, passport and the bearer shares in the Puerto Rican liquor company. He already had two plane tickets to Nassau in his jacket pocket.

The only other item of business before taking off was the meeting with the Nardini brothers that afternoon. They would hand him a certified check on a Bahamian bank to cover the week's drug take, his bearer shares and Jane's interest in Crimson Liquors. There would have to be a cash adjustment, but there were no problems about taking cash into Nassau, only a Treasury Regulation about taking cash out of the United States without declaring it. The Nardinis insisted on seeing the Crimson Liquors office and warehouse even though Callahan's preference was for the garage under the Common.

CHAPTER 30

▼

Saturday morning, Callahan put on his turtleneck outfit except for the wig and horn-rimmed glasses. He left his apartment wearing a beret and gabardine raincoat—what he would normally wear to Barney's on a wet day that was unusually cold for June. The wig and glasses were in an opaque, plastic shopping bag in case he needed a change of costume. He walked down Mass. Ave. as if he didn't have a care in the world, apparently paying no attention to anyone else on the street. Twice, however, he stopped, once to tie a shoelace that really didn't need tying, once to inspect a wicker chair in the window of a boutique—both times to check whether he was being followed.

Fortunately, Libertino and Collins had stuck to their game plan. One plainclothesman was polishing a 1950 Chevy parked in front of Callahan's apartment. The other was studying a watercolor exhibit at a sidewalk art show across the street. Neither had paid any attention to Callahan's departure, but the man being paid to polish his own car reached in through the open window on the driver's side to pick up a microphone once Callahan was safely out of sight.

"Subject has left his apartment, proceeding south on Mass. Ave towards Barney's Bookstore. Over."

"Maintain stations. Over and out," replied Collins.

✳ ✳ ✳ ✳

Jane Ransome opened the door at Barney's for Callahan. She had borrowed his key to get the store ready to open.

- 149 -

Callahan said, "Here's your plane ticket for tonight. We've got reservations at the Bluebeard in Nassau, connecting rooms. I'm not expecting any trouble, but the meeting with the Nardinis may take longer than it should. There's no reason for you to be there this afternoon. I'll meet you at the plane tonight. If I should get held up, go ahead without me. At this time of year I'll have no problem getting a flight tomorrow.

"What about the deposit slips from today's distribution?" asked Jane.

"I'll pick them up here on my way to Crimson Liquors. Have you got the deed properly executed for me?"

"Have I ever let you down?" she asked, handing him an envelope. "What about this bookstore?"

"The Nardinis are buying that, too, more as an accommodation than anything else. I understand they've worked out some new way to distribute the drugs. It's probably time the system was changed, anyhow. Are you all set to deal the keys today?" asked Callahan.

"Dan, why don't you relax? You know I've handled the job before. It's much safer if we aren't seen together."

*   *   *   *

Back at Callahan's apartment, the superintendent had left Libertino and Sullivan alone. Libertino was doing all of the searching.

"Not that I couldn't use some help," he said, "But there's an art to searching a room and getting everything back in place. Too many people leave an obvious trail. Also, when a guy thinks his place may be searched, he may arrange things in an odd way or set up a booby trap—a paper match or toothpick that will fall down inside if a drawer is opened. Callahan must not be worried about a search. I haven't seen anything of that kind in these rooms."

"Maybe there's nothing here to cause him any problems," said Sullivan.

"Here's something interesting," said Libertino. From the middle desk drawer he pulled out a black ledger about the size of a paperback novel. Inside the front cover was the legend, "Stamp Transactions of Daniel J. Callahan."

"It could be bona fide," he said. "There are six stamp albums on that table in the corner covering the United States, Canada and a variety of Caribbean islands. I leafed through all of them without finding anything suspicious."

The pages of the ledger were perfectly straightforward until the last twenty-five pages. Then the right-hand pages told a different story. There were weekly entries of figures opposite B-1, B-2, B-3 and B-4 with monthly totals that built up gradually to over two million for the last entry.

"Get your camera out, Pete," said Libertino. "I think we've hit pay dirt. Take pictures of both sides of the ledger for the last ten pages, and also the title page, the one with Callahan's name."

"What the hell does it mean?" asked Sullivan.

"I wouldn't have the foggiest idea either if I hadn't seen summaries of Crimson Liquors' deposits in four different banks. Callahan was obviously keeping track of the weekly take from the drug game to make sure that all the profits were channeled through Crimson Liquors to his Puerto Rican company."

"Why would he keep a record like this in an unlocked desk?"

"I think he was smart to hide it openly among his stamp records rather than put it in a wall safe or a locked drawer. Besides so far as he knew there was nothing to connect him with Crimson Liquors, and under normal circumstances no bank would reveal a customer's deposits."

When Sullivan had finished with the camera, Libertino wiped off the ledger and put it carefully back in the desk drawer. Sullivan pointed to the bedroom.

"Have you searched in there yet?"

"No, I was saving that for last."

"It looks like he's going on a trip," said Sullivan. "There's one of those folding canvas bags with side pockets, big enough to hold two or three suits and enough clothes for a week. He's also got a smaller bag that will fit under his airplane seat, both of them crammed to the point where the seams may burst."

It took Libertino more than an hour to search the bags carefully, removing and replacing the contents of each section one at a time. There was nothing but clothes, toilet articles and a framed Yale diploma.

"Take a picture of the diploma for Witherspoon," he said. "Then send the film back to the lab and make some prints for Collins. When you're through, I could use you back here. I intend to serve both warrants when Callahan returns. Don't forget your gun. He might turn nasty."

✴   ✴   ✴   ✴

At 12:15 Taylor reported in from the van outside Barney's: "Subject entering the bookstore. Now he's coming out, headed south on Mass. Ave. Over."

"Keep an eye on him as long as you can, but don't leave the van," said Collins. He looked at Sullivan and Witherspoon. "I think it would be a mistake to tail him now, but I sure as hell would like to know where he's going."

"He's got to go his apartment to pick up his bags," said Sullivan.

"Yeah, I know," said Collins, "but in the meantime he may be meeting some of the big fish in this game, the guys we'd really like to pull in."

Taylor's voice broke in. "Subject is turning east on Eustis Street. I've got my field glasses on him. Now he's moving out of sight behind some houses."

"The cocksucker!" said Collins. "His apartment's on the other side of Mass. Ave. He's up to something. Sullivan, you get your ass over to Crimson Liquors. Take a transceiver with you. Stay out of sight. Call in if you see anyone—especially Callahan—go in the office or warehouse."

"Who else are you expecting?" asked Sullivan.

"Maybe the Ransome dame," said Collins. "You know what she looks like, don't you?"

"A real hot tomato from her picture. I'm sure I'd recognize her. What do I do about Libertino? He told me to come back to Callahan's apartment."

"I'll square it with Joe," said Collins. "A lieutenant still gets to tell a sergeant where to get off. We'll bring in one of the men from outside the apartment, Hennessey maybe if that's where he is. I'm having trouble keeping track of everyone today."

The light over Channel 5 on Collins' radio equipment started blinking. He switched channels.

"Lynch here," said a disembodied voice. "I'm just outside the van at the end of Essex Street near South Station. We've picked up three guys already going in to the marked lockers and carrying cases away. Two out of the three relocked the empty lockers. We got 'em all padlocked to a steel rail inside the van."

"Anybody we know?" asked Collins.

"Paddy Weaver," said Lynch, knowing the news would please Collins.

"Holy shit!" said Collins. "We been trying to nail that sunnava bitch for years."

"Strange thing is the third guy doesn't seem to fit. At first he was squawking like a stuck pig, saying we couldn't do this to E. Morton Spear. Then he suddenly clams up. Refuses to let us open the attaché case which had a combination lock. Claims it's booby-trapped to blow up if anyone tries to force it. Hell, he looks more like a banker to me than a drug pusher. Here comes Jonesy with another one. I'd better get back to the locker area before some dude escapes our net. Over and out."

"Wait one cotton pickin' moment, Bill," said Collins. "Who's the Boston guy in charge there?"

"A Lieutenant Matthews, Narcotics," said Lynch, coming back on the air.

"Yeah, I know him," said Collins. "A real bruiser. Built like a brick shit house. I'd even be sorry for the pusher who tangles with him. Stop stalling and get back to your stake-out."

Charlie Witherspoon had been listening to the radio exchange between Collins and Lynch. "E. Morton Spear," he said. "Why does that name sound familiar?" He frowned in concentration. "Got it! He's connected with one of the banks Crimson Liquors deals with. He signed the covering letter for the summaries of account activity the bank sent over. Where can I find a phone to use without tying up your line?"

"Use Libertino's," said Collins. "There's nobody in his office today. You remember where it is, don't you, right across the hall?"

In Libertino's office, Charlie looked up the number of the law firm Splithair, Cavil & Quibble and dialed it. When he asked for Quibble, the switchboard operator wanted to know "Which Quibble?"

"Reginald, the younger one," said Charlie. He wondered whether there might be three generations active in the same law firm. After a brief conversation with a secretary, he got through.

"What can I do for you, Charlie? Have you run into more problems with Crimson Liquors?"

"This may be an entirely different matter," said Charlie. "Is there an E. Morton Spear connected with the bank you represent, I mean the bank with the Crimson Liquors account?"

"Certainly. He's an assistant vice-president—one of twenty-five. Why do you ask?"

"We've got him padlocked to the railing in a police wagon on Essex Street near South Station. I use the editorial 'we,' of course."

"Good lord! What's he supposed to have done?"

"The police picked him up in a South Station drug raid. He took an attaché case from one of the coin-operated lockers there in an area the police had staked out. It's all connected with the drug distribution scheme Crimson Liquors seems to be a part of."

"The bank just happens to be looking for Spear for an entirely different reason," said Quibble. "I just can't see him connected with drugs in any way."

"Why is the bank looking for Spear?" asked Witherspoon.

"I tell you this in the strictest confidence," said Quibble. "There's a stack of bearer bonds missing, more than five million dollars worth, collateral put up for a loan. Spear is one of six persons with access to the vault area where the bonds were kept."

"You think the bonds are in the attaché case Spear has with him?" asked Witherspoon.

"I wouldn't be telling you if I didn't believe it was a distinct possibility—although it's hard to believe another Yale man would betray a sacred trust."

"Wait 'til I see Conover," thought Charlie, thinking of his partner's derogatory remarks about Harvard.

"Reggie, I suggest you get over to that van with somebody from the bank who can identify those bonds and prove that the bank is entitled to hold them as collateral. Lieutenant Matthews, Narcotics, is in charge. I'll try to let him know through the Cambridge police that you're coming. If you can persuade Spear to open the case you may be able to get him out of there, assuming there are no drugs inside. I doubt if Matthew is interested in an embezzlement unless the bank wants to press charges."

"Normally the bank doesn't prosecute because it doesn't want the publicity," said Quibble. "I really appreciate what you're doing to help. We Ivy League types need to stick together."

Charlie explained the situation to Collins who was able to talk to Matthews on Hennessey's walkie-talkie.

Matthews readily agreed to release E. Morton Spear if only the bank's bonds were in the case. "You guys should see what we've turned up so far from those lockers in addition to horse and coke. There are some diamonds which the robbery detail think were taken from a Washington Street jeweler a month ago, a batch of the filthiest pictures I've ever seen, and I've seen some weird ones. One guy even kept his burglar's tools in a locker along with a black sweater, knitted cap and mask. We oughtta do a routine search of those lockers every few months."

CHAPTER 31

▼

Across the street from Crimson Liquors there was a mini park with a statue of Paul Revere, three large red maples, a bed of tulips past their prime, and a concrete bench. Pete Sullivan was sitting on the bench, doing the New York Times Crossword puzzle, but keeping a nonchalant eye on the buildings across the street. At precisely three o'clock, Callahan, wearing his wig, turtleneck sweater and horn-rimmed glasses, showed up at the office entrance.

Sullivan pretended to be absorbed in his puzzle, but he took his transceiver out from under the newspaper once Callahan was inside and turned his back to the street so that anyone watching from Crimson Liquors could not see what he was doing.

"Man in turtleneck sweater, bushy hair and horn-rimmed glasses entering Crimson Liquors," he said. "Fits description of Fleming you gave me. Over."

"Pete—stay put, and watch closely for anyone else going in to that building. I'm sending Taylor and the van over. There's another man in the van, and you'll be able to cover the place better. Got your gun?"

"Sure thing. Libertino warned me to pick it up. Said we might be making an arrest. Over and out."

At the station, Collins looked at Witherspoon. "That reminds me. We might as well let Joe in on the kill. He phoned me an hour ago and gave me the unlisted number at Callahan's apartment."

Sullivan's voice came in on the radio again to report two men in funny-looking suits entering the office. Their tailor in Milan would have been incensed to hear his description of the suits. Collins picked up the phone to call Libertino.

"Joe, Witherspoon and me have been studying the prints Pete made from the film he shot this morning. I think we got enough to book Callahan on a drug charge."

Libertino said, "Let's make it Murder One, too. That way he's got no chance to get bail."

"I'm sending the van over to Crimson Liquors where Callahan is now. They'll pick you up on the way. Think you can handle the arrest?"

"You betcha," said Libertino. "This is one I'm looking forward to."

*   *   *   *

Inside Crimson Liquors things were going smoothly. The Nardini brothers had been given a quick tour of the warehouse. It was half empty. There really wasn't much to see except neatly stacked cartons of liquor. Callahan explained that the inventory system was all computer controlled. They could rely on the computer printout to accurately list the stock as of that afternoon. He was confident that the Nardinis would not insist on a physical count. There simply wasn't time.

"You're getting a bargain on the scotch and bourbon," he said. "Wholesale prices have gone up ten percent since we bought the stuff."

"That's enough propaganda," said Guiseppe. "We're paying a good price for the building which we financed at ridiculously low interest rates. What's the total on today's deposits?"

Callahan handed over an envelope thick with deposit slips. "I make it slightly over a million, five."

Giovanni took out his pocket calculator to check the figures. "We'll round it off at $2,100,000. That includes $450,000 for this building and the inventory, and $100,000 for the bearer shares in the Puerto Rican company."

"What form is the payment in?" asked Callahan.

"We've got a cashier's check drawn on Barclay's Bank—it has a branch in Nassau—and a personal check for the balance."

"Satisfactory," said Callahan.

"All we need now," said Giuseppe, "is the deed to the property and your bearer shares in the Alvarez Company. Then we can both get going."

Callahan handed over the documents. "I'll leave first. You two wait for another five minutes. Don't forget to lock up. That booze is well worth stealing."

Callahan walked out of the office door right into the arms of Joe Libertino and Pete Sullivan.

Just then Jane Ransome drove by in a VW Rabbit. She had been about to pull into the Crimson Liquors' parking area to clean out her desk. When she saw Callahan being arrested, she kept on going.

The Nardini brothers also caught a glimpse of the arrest from the office window and hightailed it for the warehouse exit where Taylor was waiting. He was happy to escort them to the van and handcuff them to a railing inside the rear section. When he saw Callahan approaching in the custody of Libertino and wearing his wig, turtleneck sweater and horn-rimmed glasses, Taylor said, "You're the guy who led Riley such a merry chase on the Red Line."

Libertino showed Callahan the search warrant.

They left Taylor behind to comb Crimson Liquors' records for further evidence of Puerto Rican connections. Then they stopped off at Callahan's apartment to pick up his stamp book record. Libertino and Sullivan put on a convincing show of looking in several other places first.

Back at the station personal searches produced all of the documents that had changed hands at the Crimson Liquors meeting plus a closing memo in Giuseppe's handwriting allocating the items covered by the $2,100,000, tying the checks found on Callahan to the ownership documents found on the Nardinis. Callahan's passport and plane ticket were also discovered.

Collins told Sullivan, "Get an APB out on that Ransome dame. Go to the airport yourself tonight. She'll probably try to catch the same flight to Nassau. Bring her in."

*   *   *   *

An hour later, while Collins and Libertino were still questioning Callahan, Taylor came in with the clincher. He found a Crimson Liquors file that showed extensive credit memos to the Puerto Rican company for return goods. Witherspoon got first crack at the file.

"I can't believe it," he said. "If we can believe these figures, the Alvarez outfit sent back about half the stuff they bought. The operation was bigger than we thought. Crimson Liquors sold at close to its cost, but that scheme couldn't transfer money fast enough, so they simply gave credit for fictitious returns. The IRS will be fascinated."

Callahan restrained a groan, but his face showed that the remark had cut close to the bone. He stuck to a simple story, refusing to ask for a lawyer. He was merely handling a business transaction for a friend. The deed betrayed the fact that she was the owner of Crimson Liquors so he wasn't giving anything away.

Since the shares in the Alvarez Company were bearer shares, and the checks were payable to a Bahamian bank to be credited to a numbered account, there was nothing with his name on it.

Finally Collins and Libertino called it a day. They sent Callahan to a detention cell.

"We'd better get him up for a state judge in the morning," said Collins. "We don't want to give him an out. I better talk to the feds in case they want to take over—unless you think we got him on the murder rap."

"I'm afraid we haven't enough evidence to convict, although I'm more than satisfied that he killed Fisher. His eyes gave him away several times while we were questioning him. This guy is no hardened criminal. Let's get him arraigned before a state judge and keep our options open. Talk to the feds, too."

"He may be no hardened criminal," said Collins, "But he sure as hell caused a lot of misery, not to mention at least three deaths."

Libertino said, "Since he won't get the chair anyhow, what difference does it make whether he does twenty years for murder or dealing drugs? Crazy as it sounds, he'd be more likely to get parole on a murder conviction."

Charlie Witherspoon stood up. "Unless you need me for something more, I plan to make an early night of it and catch a morning plane back to Chicago. I'm not sure I'll come back for another reunion."

"You Harvard types come in handy sometimes," said Collins generously.

"Seekers of truth, that's what we try to be," said Charlie, thinking it wasn't a bad exit line for a man who had spent eleven years becoming the epitome of a Harvard man.

CHAPTER 32

▼

When Charlie got back to Tom's apartment, he found him and John Rogers sipping away at gins and tonic and eager to find out what had happened. Charlie filled them in on the events of the day, stopping occasionally for a drink from his own scotch highball.

Tom said, "I don't understand how a school teacher with Callahan's background and education could get mixed up in the dirty business of distributing drugs."

"Since Callahan's decided to clam up, we can only speculate," said Charlie. "I think he may have been trying to get back at a society with a warped sense of values. Many entertainers—actors, professional athletes—make more money in one year, sometimes in one performance, than the average school teacher makes in a lifetime."

"What does Collins think?" asked Tom. "Hasn't he been a regular customer at Barney's for years? He must have some idea of what the guy was doing."

"It's Collins' theory I was just starting to explain," said Charlie. "I gather that Callahan's pension from the school where he taught was almost nothing. It was integrated with Social Security so that as the federal monthly payments increased with inflation, the private payments decreased. Even with the income from the bookstore he was living on the edge of poverty. When the opportunity to make some real money came along, he just couldn't resist it. I suspect that he was approached to let his bookstore be used as a distribution point, but I'll bet the refinements of the system, the musical code and use of the public lockers, were his brainchild. Also he knew people in the book trade like Roxy who proved useful."

"Incidentally, I received my usual fifty dollars this morning," said John Rogers. "It came by mail for a change."

"I think Callahan was trying to avoid any unnecessary contacts before he left the country. He had reservations on a flight to the Bahamas tonight."

"I admit the money came in handy," said Rogers, "but I'm damned glad it's over. I really haven't been able to sleep well since I was beaten up, and I've been having all sorts of guilt feelings about the money."

"If you want to give it away, I know of a specially deserving charity," said Tom.

"I don't feel that guilty," said John.

"One thing that still bugs me," said Tom, "is why the syndicate, or whatever you want to call them, would risk leaving hundreds of thousands of dollars worth of drugs in public lockers. You could design your own master key by renting four or five lockers, tracing the keys, and coming up with a single pattern that would open all the locks. Those locker keys are pretty simple things."

"That's part of the beauty of the scheme," said Charlie. "The average crook thinks the way you do. If it's easy to get to, it can't be worth much. Remember, the stuff is in the lockers less than twelve hours. Anyone watching the lockers being loaded would have no reason to believe the attaché cases contained anything other than business papers."

John Rogers said, "I've read that diamond merchants operate on a similar philosophy, mailing gems by ordinary parcel post with no insurance or registration marks to show that the contents are valuable."

"Exactly," said Charlie. "Of course the parcels are insured, under a special policy that requires the shipper to notify the insurance company weekly of the details of the shipments, but as you say there's nothing on the package to show that it's insured. One of the big insurance companies told me their losses had been less than one-half of one per cent of the value shipped."

Tom went into his bedroom and came back wearing a tie and a lightweight linen sport coat. "I'll say goodbye now if you don't mind. I'm unlikely to be around when you leave for the airport in the morning."

"Where do you expect to be?" asked Charlie.

"Let me just say that thanks to good police work this afternoon, the danger is over and a better selection of roommates has become available."

"Give Tina my very best," said Charlie. "John, how about joining me for dinner at *Le Plat d'Argent*?"

"I'd be delighted," said John. "It'll be the first free meal I've had this year."

"I'll use your phone to make a reservation. Then I should call the Dean to let him know his worries are over. I won't tell him that I still have nagging doubts about the cheating."

THE END

978-0-595-37231-7
0-595-37231-7

Printed in the United States
38655LVS00006B/115

9 780595 372317